Cooperman House

Cooperman House

TIM BROWN

RESOURCE *Publications* · Eugene, Oregon

COOPERMAN HOUSE

Resource Publications
An Imprint of Wipf and Stock Publishers
199 W. 8th Ave., Suite 3
Eugene, OR 97401

www.wipfandstock.com

PAPERBACK ISBN: 978-1-6667-4177-3
HARDCOVER ISBN: 978-1-6667-4178-0
EBOOK ISBN: 978-1-6667-4179-7

MARCH 30, 2022 8:04 AM

Contents

Dedication

P ARANORMAL SURPRISES ALWAYS HOLD us captive for a moment. *Did that door shut by itself?*

People surprise us too. Consider my writer's group – a talented assortment of kind, bright, people who allow me to pass my ideas through their clarifying prism of new possibilities each month. I am never surprised by their honesty. I am always surprised by their unselfishness. This book is dedicated to them: Marlis Broadhead, Dick Brown, Joyce Brown (may she rest in peace), Frank Cook, Gregg Coonrod, Charlotte Henderson, Shawn Parkison, Kent Moore, and Adam Sales.

Cooperman House is a better story because of their guidance. I hope it holds you captive for moment.

Bells and Chimes

1

CRIMINAL CASES ARRIVE ON my desk as illicit jigsaw puzzles waiting to be assembled one uniquely shaped piece at a time. If pieces are missing, I find myself chasing ghosts. My first supernatural predicament occurred even before I joined the FBI. I think of it whenever someone asks about the toy car that sits on my credenza beside my wife's picture. It was a gift from Lawrence, our friend and neighbor when I was a student at Denver University.

"Bells and chimes are going to ring. Mamie Eisenhower, Mamie Eisenhower, Mamie Eisenhower," Lawrence intoned each morning as he walked past our house. About eight o'clock, I'd hear his Gregorian chant start slow and low and built to a pinnacled pitch on the word *ring*, then lower into a monotone ripple of the former First Lady's name three times in rapid succession. Lawrence became my morning habit. At first, he was entertainment. Eventually, he was a friend who helped us come to grips with an invisible visitor to our new home.

It was late summer in 1978. We'd only been in Denver about three weeks, as I was starting a two-year graduate program in forensic psychology. My wife, Connie, was teaching fourth grade. It was her first job. Our recent marriage, my full-ride scholarship, her new job, and the unique one-bedroom apartment we'd found all seemed to fold into a predetermined plan. And Lawrence was a little something extra.

The apartment came with a bird's-eye view of our enigmatic neighbor. On week-ends, we'd enjoy our coffee on our second-story balcony and watch Lawrence hurry past in a world all his own. We heard him coming from half block away. He wore blue denim overalls with badly frayed cuffs that draped behind his orange, high-top tennis shoes. About thirty years old, slightly bent, and round shouldered, he stared straight forward beneath his Broncos ball cap. His quick, short, orange-shoed steps kept cadence with his chant. It never varied. "Bells and chimes are going to ring. Mamie Eisenhower, Mamie Eisenhower, Mamie Eisenhower."

Verse after repetitious verse, separated by a few seconds of silence, accompanied him past our house and all the way to the corner. His first stop was usually the neighborhood drugstore, which was a right turn at the corner and just up the street. That's where I learned his name when I heard the clerk speak to him. I had an early-morning meeting with my sociology professor and stopped at Glazier's Pharmacy to pick up Connie's asthma inhaler and eye-glass cleaning solution. I stood in line directly behind Lawrence.

"Hey, Lawrence. How ya doin?" the smiling, middle-aged clerk and store manager asked. Her reading glasses rested on her ample bosom, suspended from a delicate silver chain. Her name tag read Matty.

"Good, good, good. Good, good, good," Lawrence responded, as he placed two candy bars on the counter.

"Butterfinger and Cherry Mash, I'll bet." Matty said.

"Yes, a Butterfinger and Cherry Mash. Butterfinger and Cherry Mash," Lawrence repeated. "Charge please. Charge please. Charge please."

"You got it, Lawrence. Tell your Momma hello for me, will you? How's she feeling."

"She fine, she fine, she fine," Lawrence said and hurried out the door.

I hesitated, then asked, "Lawrence is quite a guy, isn't he?" I placed my items on the worn counter along with my student ID. The store offered a 10 percent discount to college students.

"Oh my, yes. We all love him," the cheerful clerk responded as she placed her half-frame readers on the bridge of her nose to examine my ID card. "Ronald McCall, is it? New to the neighborhood?"

"Yes. We've been here about three weeks."

"Welcome. I'm Matty."

"Couldn't help but notice Lawrence. He passes by our house every day singing about bells and chimes and Mamie Eisenhower. What's that about? Do you know?"

"Don't know the full story. There's some connection between Mamie Eisenhower and his dad's funeral. I'm sure it all makes sense to Lawrence. He doesn't miss much, and he forgets nothing."

That was our first clue Lawrence was more than a neighbor with a developmental disability. He was a neighborhood favorite. Almost everyone knew him and shared at least partial responsibility for his wellbeing. In return, Lawrence helped an aging neighborhood of disconnected contrasts become a community. Our apartment was in a once proud but still prominent old home in a timeworn Denver neighborhood. The house was built in 1920 by the owners of Cooperman's Department Store. By 1978, when we lived there, the home had been converted into two units. We lived upstairs. The larger, first-floor flat was occupied by the owners, Terrance and Margarite Tucker.

Our living room had been the master bedroom of the original house and included a small fireplace and a walkout balcony. In its heyday the five-block stretch of Jackson Street was an upscale collection of homes for the wealthy. Today, most of the grand old homes had been replaced by modest bungalows, Tudors, and a few newer ranches. The inconsistent collection of houses added to the importance of Cooperman House and its ever-present nod to another era.

We were lucky to find the place. We liked its history, and we were learning to like the neighborhood, including our chanting neighbor. We wanted to know more about him. By my cautious standards, Connie was inappropriately curious at times. I was satisfied to let things unfold at their own pace. She wanted to learn Lawrence's story right away. She sped me up, and I slowed her down.

By late September, the air chilled, and on a Saturday morning we awoke to a peaceful blanket of early Colorado snow. It was a beautiful surprise, which stood in stark contrast to the event that allowed us to learn more about Lawrence. That morning he dressed for the snow. He sported an orange and blue Broncos jacket. His Broncos ball cap became a Broncos stocking cap, and his orange tennis shoes became insulated work boots with orange laces. His frayed overalls didn't change. Neither did his morning Mamie Eisenhower chant.

The first snow always awoke my inner child. We needed tissues, shaving cream and a newspaper, and it was a perfect morning for a walk in the snow. I left the apartment for Glazier's Pharmacy about five minutes after we heard Lawrence's chant fade past the corner. His were the only tracks in two inches of fresh snow. As I rounded the corner toward the drugstore, I saw a mound on the edge of the sidewalk wearing a Broncos jacket. It was half a block away. I ran to him.

"Lawrence, Lawrence! Are you alright?" I yelled as I ran, eventually skidding up to him as if I had just stolen second base. "Lawrence. You okay?" He lay on his side with his back toward me. His left arm and his face were splayed against the snow.

"Leg hurt. Leg hurt. Leg hurt," Lawrence muttered.

"Okay, buddy. Can you roll toward me?"

He shifted his weight and moaned, "Hurt, hurt, hurt."

"Okay, buddy. Don't move. I'll get help." I took off my jacket, made a pillow of it, and placed it between his face and the snow-covered grass. "I'll be right back."

Glazier's Pharmacy was thirty yards away. I ran with abbreviated strides to avoid slipping and burst through the door yelling, "I need help. Lawrence has fallen. He's injured. Please help!"

My panicked scan of the store immediately calmed when it landed on Matty's familiar face. "What happened? Where is he?" she asked.

"Don't know what happened, but he's lying in the snow just up the street. He's in too much pain to move. Call an ambulance. I'm going back to be with him."

"Hold on," Matty said. She yelled at the pharmacist, who stood behind the pharmacy counter toward the near side of the store. "Ralph, you getting all this?"

"Got it," Ralph answered as he picked up the phone.

"Go!" Matty said to me.

I ran back to Lawrence, who had not changed his position. "Lawrence, help is on the way. Help is on the way," I said as I panted. "Can you tell me again where you hurt?"

"Leg hurt. Man hit," he answered.

"A man hit you?"

"Hit, hit, hit."

"Which leg? This one?" I asked as I reached down and touched his right ankle.

"No. Other. Other. Other."

I heard Matty's soothing voice, as she shuffled toward us through the snow, wearing a knee-length wool coat, but no boots. Her black, orthopedic shoes seemed vulnerable yet defiant in the snow. "Lawrence, Lawrence, Lawrence," she said calmly. Her maternal presence was absolutely reassuring.

"It's his left leg. He said a man hit him. Can you believe that?" I asked in disbelief.

Matty resisted my invitation to become angry. "Lawrence?" she asked as she took a candy bar from her coat pocket. "How about a Butterfinger?"

"Too cold," Lawrence murmured. "Too cold, too cold."

"Okay, I'll save it for later."

His grimaced whisper followed, "Charge please, charge please, charge please."

"This one's on me, Lawrence. You said someone hit you. Do you know who it was?"

"A man. Took cap. Took wallet. Smelled bad."

A blaring siren interrupted the conversation from two blocks away.

"Hear that, Lawrence? Someone's coming to help you. They'll take you to the hospital and make your leg feel better. Is it just your leg that hurts?" Matty asked.

"Leg, leg, leg."

"I want to make sure I understood you, Lawrence. All you noticed was how he smelled?"

"Smelled bad, smelled bad, smelled bad," Lawrence said.

The siren stopped as the ambulance pulled to the curb with red lights flashing. Two paramedics climbed out and assessed the situation. They carefully rolled Lawrence onto a flat board, placed a splint on his left leg, lifted him onto a gurney, and loaded him into the ambulance. One of them picked up my snow-covered jacket and asked whose it was. I claimed it and told them what we knew about Lawrence's difficulty. Matty asked to ride to the hospital with them. Recognizing the value of a familiar face at Lawrence's side, the paramedics agreed.

"Where we taking him?" Matty asked.

"Denver General," the paramedic answered.

"Mr. McCall. Would you go back to the store and tell Ralph where I've gone? Also, tell him to call Lawrence's mom and tell her what's going on."

"Sure," I said, surprised she remembered my name. I did as she asked and then hurried home without tissues, shaving cream or a newspaper.

Stay Fearless

2

C ONNIE LISTENED CAREFULLY TO the story of Lawrence's mugging. She was as concerned as I was, and now we had even more Lawrence questions. We learned his last name when a detective came to our door later that day.

"Hello, I'm Sergeant Bloomfield," said the large, friendly man wearing a brown leather bomber jacket and tweed flat cap. He flashed his badge and asked. "Are you Ronald McCall?"

"Yes. I'm Ron McCall."

"I understand you were first on the scene of the Lawrence Stroud incident. I'd like to talk with you about it."

"Please come in."

Bloomfield took off his flat cap and placed in on the divan as he sat down beside it. Even beneath a jacket, his muscular frame was conspicuous. Without his pleasant smile, he could have been intimidating. His tentative position toward the leading edge of the cushion suggested his interview wouldn't take long.

I introduced him to Connie and gave him an overview of what happened. I explained we didn't really know Lawrence and assured him Lawrence wouldn't know us from Adam.

"We're new in the neighborhood. I'm a student at DU," I explained. "We were aware of him because he walks by here every morning singing. It was pure coincidence I found him and could call him by name."

"How'd you know his name?"

"Matty, the clerk at Glazier's told me," I said. "If there's a hero in all this, it's Matty. She was unflappable."

"Yes, we know Matty. Everyone does. She's as much a neighborhood fixture as Lawrence. But we're not looking for a hero. We're looking for the person who did this. As you may have figured out, Lawrence is special. That's particularly true for those of us on the force. His dad was a cop and was killed while on duty years back. We've all kept a kind eye on Lawrence ever since.

"So, you saw nobody fleeing from the scene or tracks in the snow or other evidence?" Sergeant Bloomfield asked.

"No. There may have been tracks, but I didn't notice. I wanted to get help."

"We checked the scene. The ambulance guys, you, and Matty pretty much did a number on footprints, though there were some that were clear and distinct. We've taken pictures. Would you mind showing me the shoes you wore so I can an identify your footprints and narrow things down."

I retrieved my duck boots and handed them to him. "So, how is Lawrence? Do you know? Still in the hospital?"

"Yeah, still there. Probably be home tomorrow. His leg was broken. But it looks like he's going to be okay."

"Things like this happen often in this neighborhood?" Connie asked.

"No, they don't. They really don't."

"Seems a lot of work for a stocking cap and a wallet that probably didn't have much in it," Connie said.

"Yes, ma'am."

"What'd they hit him with?"

"We aren't sure, ma'am."

"Have you talked with him?" Connie asked.

"Yes, yesterday."

"What'd he say? Could he identify who hit him?"

"No. That's why I'm here. All he said about the guy was he smelled bad."

"Smelled bad. Like what?"

"Lawrence didn't say. Must have been a smell he couldn't identify by name."

"Where's he live anyway. We'd like to visit him when he gets home."

"I'm not free to tell you, ma'am."

I knew Connie would pepper the detective with more questions until I sidetracked her. "We can talk with Matty about that. I'll bet she knows. Of course, we'd like to check on Lawrence, unless there's a reason for us to keep our distance."

"Yes, talk to Matty," Bloomfield said. "Do you have other boots you can wear? I'd like to take these to photograph the tread. I'll have them back tomorrow."

"Yes, of course. Take them."

"Thank you. If you think of anything else that might help us, please call me directly," he handed me his business card. Then he surprised me with a personal question. "So, Mr. McCall, what are you studying, high finance?"

"No, far from it. I'm doing graduate work in forensic psychology."

"Oh, no kidding. Going to be a crime stopper too, are you?"

"Hope so," I said.

"Great. Welcome to the club."

Sergeant Rodrick Bloomfield tied the boot laces together and slung them over his shoulder, smiled, touched the bill of his cap, and walked down the stairs to his black, unmarked car.

"Well, it's good to know Lawrence won't be just another mugging to the police," I said. "Do we have the number for Glazier's. Think it's too soon to call Matty?"

"Not at all. Call her. If you don't, I will," Connie answered. "Glazier's number is on my inhaler box."

I called immediately, certain that Connie's insistence would not cease until I did. Matty answered and I quickly briefed her on the police visit. She already knew more than we did.

"Lawrence's lower leg is broken. The big bone. It's not too bad and should heal fast, they say. They'll cast him up tomorrow after the swelling goes down. I suppose he'll be home late tomorrow. No surgery necessary, but he'll be slowed for a while."

"Where's he live?"

"Just a couple blocks or so from you. Straight north on Jackson. It's a big, old home from a different era. Sort of like your place. You live in the Cooperman House, right?"

"Yes. Upstairs apartment."

"Thought so. Noticed the address on your wife's prescription." Like Lawrence, Matty didn't miss much.

"We'd like to visit him. Any reason that's not a good idea?"

"None at all. Call first. Let his mom know you're coming. But he'd be glad to see you. And he'll remember you, I'll bet. If he doesn't, just tell him where you live. I told him you were the new folks in the Cooperman House. He knows that old the place very well."

"Is that so?"

Matty gave me the Stroud's phone number and address. I thanked her and asked one more question. "Matty, did he say anything about who attacked him?"

"Not much. Lawrence was pretty upset so they let me stay while the detective talked with him. Thought I'd calm him some. What Lawrence remembered most was the man's odor. He said it was a man in a hooded sweatshirt. But he kept saying he smelled bad. The rotten bastard must have taken Lawrence totally by surprise. You know how he walks. He marches. He stares straight ahead and marches."

"Yeah, and on a snowy morning, he was probably even more focused on his next step forward," I said.

"From what we could piece together, it looks like the guy must have come from the street side. Slammed Lawrence's leg with a metal rod or something. Robbed him and fled. The guy seemed to know Lawrence kept his wallet in the bib pocket on his overalls. He went straight for it. Probably grabbed the stocking cap as an afterthought and ran."

"Damn. Someone who knew him, maybe? That's someplace to start, I guess. We'll let him get settled in at home and then go see him. I'll keep you posted if I learn anything new. You too, I hope. Thank you, Matty."

"You're welcome, Ron. I can call you Ron, right?

"Sure, you can."

"I've got a question for you."

"Shoot."

"How do you like Cooperman House so far?"

"We love it. It's perfect for us. Even has a tiny fireplace. Plus, there's a small, finished attic room that's perfect for studying."

"That's great. Nice to have you in the neighborhood. I've got a customer. Gotta go. We'll talk soon."

It didn't strike me as odd that Matty was interested in our opinion of the apartment until I told Connie about our conversation. Even then, I dismissed it as neighborly small talk. Connie wasn't so sure.

Two days after the attack we called and went to Lawrence's home. His mother, Helen Stroud, greeted us at the front door, "Welcome, we are delighted you've come. Please come in." Helen Stroud was an energetic woman in her mid-fifties. She was gracious and at the same time cheerfully protective of her son. "Lawrence looks forward to meeting you," she said, directing us to the living room of their well-kept Victorian home. As Matty said, it was one of the other homes from yesteryear that graced the neighborhood.

"Look who's here, Lawrence. It's the McCalls, Ron and Connie. Ron is the man who helped you when you went down in the snow. Do you remember?"

Lawrence's left leg was in a knee-high cast and propped up on an antique hassock with mahogany legs and needlepoint upholstery. He glanced our way, though he didn't look at us. His eyes swung past us and landed on the green velvet drapes encasing the front window. "Member, member, member," he said.

"Hello again, Lawrence," I said. "You look like you're feeling better than the last time I saw you."

"Please sit down, you two. Can I get you something, coffee, tea?" his mother asked.

"Oh, no thank you. Not for me," I said. Connie smiled and shook her head as we sat down on the mohair divan. "We won't stay long. We just wanted to see how Lawrence is doing and give him this." I handed him a tissue-topped bag.

Lawrence opened it quickly. He took out a brand-new Denver Broncos stocking cap and pulled it down over the tops of his ears, smiled, pointed at me, and said, "Coop, Coop, Coop!"

His mother explained. "He knows where you live. He keeps track of things like that, and he loves the Cooperman

House. He had a good friend who lived there. Like it or not, I'm afraid you have a new nickname."

"I love it. What about Connie? She get a nickname too?" I asked, looking at Lawrence.

"Connie Coop, Connie Coop, Connie Coop," Lawrence said.

We all laughed. Connie and I were delighted to discover someone beyond orange tennis shoes and a strange chant. Of course, it wasn't a surprise to his mother. Lawrence enjoyed the spotlight and seemed to want more. He bent forward and slapped his left knee three times just above his cast.

"He wants you to sign his cast," his mother said. She handed me a Sharpie, and I went to my knee to place my autograph on the fresh plaster. I signed "Coop," placing tiny initials beside the boldly printed nickname. Connie followed my lead and signed "Connie Coop." We weren't the first to sign. Matty's name was already there, plus someone named Sam.

"Lawrence, I'm surprised you know where we live. We see you walk by every morning but didn't know you saw us. Gosh, you've got to get better soon. We'll miss your singing. Mamie Eisenhower is a great way to start the day."

"Bells and chimes are going to ring, Mamie Eisenhower, Mamie Eisenhower, Mamie Eisenhower," Lawrence chanted.

Helen Stroud stood, left the living room for a moment, and returned with a large scrapbook, which she placed on the coffee table. She leafed through it, and said, "This may interest you." She pushed it toward our end of the table. We were presented with a carefully folded front page of the *Denver Post*. Unfolded, two major stories shared the page. The headline for the larger story read, Slain Detective's Life Celebrated. It chronicled the life of Lawrence's father and the details of his memorial service. Sergeant Blyth Stroud's handsome image in his dress uniform greeted us from the yellowing page. It was published on

November 14, 1957. Alongside was a story, with photo, about Mamie Eisenhower's sixty-first birthday and her work with The American Heart Association.

"A bell pealed fifteen times at the church that day, one strike for each year of Blyth's service," Mrs. Stroud explained. "Lawrence was ten years old when his father died. The chimes and this clipping connected his dad to Mamie Eisenhower, and he has never let go of it, and we wouldn't have it any other way."

"Some things should never be forgotten, right Lawrence?" I asked.

"Coop, Coop, Coop," Lawrence said.

"Mrs. Stroud, thanks so much for letting us visit. I've jotted down my phone number. If we can help you and Lawrence in any way, please call us. I'm a student at DU with a wide-open schedule, so I can probably find a way to jump in if you need me," I said as I handed her a note card with our name and number. Then I walked over to Lawrence to give him an encouraging pat on his shoulder and a word of encouragement. He winced and dodged my hand. I stepped back and looked at his mother.

"Lawrence isn't comfortable with the touch of other people," Mrs. Stroud explained. "It's alright, Ron. You had no way of knowing. And Lawrence is just fine. Aren't you Lawrence?"

"Just fine. Lawrence just fine."

"I'm sorry Lawrence. But promise me you'll heal quickly," I said. "And have your mom call us if she needs anything."

"Ron, I may do that," she answered for him. "You're very kind. Lawrence, thank them for your new cap."

"Thank you, thank you, thank you," Lawrence said.

"You're welcome, Lawrence. It looks great on you," I said. "Heal fast and come see us."

"Coop, Coop, Coop," Lawrence said.

As we walked down the sidewalk toward home, Connie spoke first. "You were wonderful. You guided the conversation to Lawrence's chant, and we found out exactly what we wanted to know. Very nice work."

"And you said almost nothing?"

"No need to. You had it covered. More important, I think you've made a friend."

"I think we both have, Connie Coop."

"Has a nice ring to it doesn't it? I kind of like it."

"Speaking of detectives, I wonder how the investigation is going? You know, Bloomfield still has my duck boots. Maybe I should call him." We were interrupted by another new neighbor.

The house just north of ours sat on a corner lot. The yard of the stucco Tudor home was immaculate. The season's first snow had melted, and a gray-haired man was taking advantage of the moist soil to edge his sidewalk. He stepped off the walk as we passed.

"Morning," I said. "Your yard's looking great."

"Morning. Yeah, I try to keep up with it. You the new Cooperman House folks?"

"Yes. I'm Ron. This is Connie."

"I'm Art, Art Mingus. Heard you're the guy who rescued Lawrence?"

"Rescued? I found him lying in the snow and got help. That's all. We just visited him. He seems to be doing fine. Do you know Lawrence?"

"Oh, yeah. Can't live around here and not know Lawrence."

"If I can ask, how'd you know I helped him?'

"Cynthia told me. She lives across the street in that little bungalow," Art said, pointing to the house.

"Gosh, news travels fast around here."

"I guess it does, especially when it comes to Lawrence. Glad to hear he's doing well."

"Yes, we are too. Well, we'll let you get back to it. Nice meeting you, Art. We'll see you again, I'm sure."

"Nice to meet you too. You guys plan to be here a while?"

"Looks that way. I'm in school at DU for a couple years."

"Well, good. Good to know. Stay fearless and enjoy the neighborhood."

"Thanks, Art."

We continued our short walk home. "Well, you've made another new friend today and found out you're famous. How about that?" Connie said.

"That was weird, wasn't it? The whole conversation was weird. 'Stay fearless and enjoy the neighborhood.' What a strange thing to say."

Cocktail Hour

3

W E BEGAN OUR FIRST-SEMESTER routine. Connie left every morning in her '75 VW Bug at seven-thirty sharp. My first class wasn't util nine on Monday, Wednesday, and Friday. Tuesday and Thursday, I was free until noon. I had more Cooperman House time than Connie, and I spent most of it in the little upstairs, dormered room, sometimes reading, sometimes banging away on my old Underwood manual typewriter. It was as heavy as a boat anchor and just as durable. Connie had an electric Smith Corona, but it was too sensitive for me. I needed something I could pound. The Underwood's bullet-proof keyboard took all the punishment I could dish out. Plus, I enjoyed the authoritative sound of its carriage return bell. Each time I finished a line, it made me feel like I had done something modestly important. We called it the upper room. We furnished it with a small desk, a reading lamp, and a bookcase. That little room, Connie's inhaler, and our TV remote control aroused suspicions we were not alone.

Connie's asthma wasn't serious enough to require inhaler use every day and a new one normally lasted for about three months. Oddly, the one I purchased for her just one week earlier had gone dry. After work, she took it back to Glazier's Pharmacy. I was in the upper room when she came home.

"Ron, can you take a little break?" Connie yelled up the stairs. "I have an inhaler story to tell you."

"Sure, I'm at a stopping point. I'll be right there. A what kind of story?"

"Just come down. You need to hear this."

She met me at the stairway door, took me by the hand, and led me to the divan. "Please sit," she said. I did and she joined me.

"Did you say inhaler story?" I asked.

"Yes, I did. I returned the empty one to Glazier's."

"And?"

"The pharmacist, Ralph's his name, right?"

"Right," I said.

"He examined the bad one, typed a new label, and gave me a new one immediately, with an apology. He was as baffled as we were. He's going to look into it."

"Well, now. That's quite a story," I said, sarcastically.

"I'm not done yet. I explained my problem to Matty on my way in, and she sent me back to talk to Ralph. As I left, she asked me if he was able to help me. I showed her the new one, and told her Ralph had no idea why the first one went bad. She had an idea of her own. She said, 'Well, it's beyond me. Unless it's that darned house."

"House?"

"Yes. This house."

"What's this house have to do with it?"

Connie hesitated, "She claims it's haunted!"

"Come on."

"That's what she said. The house and, more specifically, our apartment. She said half the people who've lived here have reported some kind of paranormal activity."

"Come on, Connie. She was pulling your leg."

"That's what I thought too. I laughed at her and told her to stop but she wouldn't budge. She claimed she didn't really believe the stories but was simply reporting what other renters told her. Then she assured me nobody's been pushed off the balcony or anything. But they've noticed strange things happening and learned to live with it or move on.

"I made a lame joke about filling the inhaler with mace to scare the next ghost away. She smiled, and then she apologized for mentioning it, although she was sure we'd hear about it from someone."

I stood and walked to the fireplace. "So, some wheezing, asthmatic spirit snuck into the bathroom last night and sucked all the goodie out of your inhaler? Is that what you're telling me?"

"No. I'm telling you what Matty told me. She said we should talk with Mr. and Mrs. Tucker. She was sure they knew about it."

"The Tuckers know about it?"

"That's what she said."

"Only met them once. The day we rented the place."

"I know. They're never outside. Waved at her a couple times. Never see him."

"And just how do we start the conversation? Hello, Mrs. Tucker. Seen any ghosts around here? Some of our medicine has come up missing and we think a spook took it."

"You're not helping at all."

"We answered the Mamie Eisenhower question. I'll bet we figure this one out too."

That night, when we turned in, I noticed Connie move her inhaler from the medicine cabinet to the drawer in our bedside table. Our rent was due in a couple of days. I decided to pay it early and see what the Tuckers had to say.

The next day, I stood at their front door and stared at the doorbell for a few moments. Then I slipped the rent envelope through the mail slot and walked away. I didn't have the courage to ask them about hauntings.

A week later, there were other supernatural nudges. The remote control for our television set went missing. "Where's the remote?" Connie asked, as she settled in to watch *Mork & Mindy*. We'd eaten out and hurried home to watch our favorite sitcom.

"Should be right there on the end table," I answered.

"I know, but it's not."

"That's odd," I said, as I walked to the set and turned it on and selected the channel manually. We chuckled our way through the thirty-minute show, sure the missing remote would turn up, and it did, but not in a place that made sense. Connie went to the kitchen to make tea and found it tucked alongside the knives in our silverware drawer.

"Okay, wise guy," she shouted. "Why did you do that?"

"Do what?"

"Put the remote in the silverware drawer."

"I did no such thing," I said.

"Come on. This is not the time for one of your goofy practical jokes."

"Honestly, Connie, I didn't touch the remote. I didn't do it," I insisted, though I understood her suspicion. I pranked her from time to time, but this was not one of those times. The inhaler mystery was too fresh for a supernatural practical joke. Even I knew that.

"Well, then how did it make its way into our silverware drawer?"

"I have no idea?" We stared at one another, afraid to say what we were thinking.

"Time to talk to the Tuckers," she said.

"Tomorrow we will." We planned to call them the next day, after we got home.

It was a Wednesday. Connie came home early to gather her thoughts before the pending conversation with the Tuckers. She heard me typing on my trusty Underwood. She chose not to interrupt me, sat and read the newspaper, and then poked around in the kitchen as she planned dinner. She was shocked when I walked through the front door.

"Where'd you go? I didn't hear you leave?" she asked.

"What? I just got here. You know I have class on Wednesday afternoon."

"I know you do. But you were here. You were upstairs typing when I got home."

"Connie. Listen to me. I just now walked in. I was in class until four. I stopped to buy gas and came home. What in the world are you talking about?"

"I am not kidding. I got home early. I heard you typing, decided not to bother you, and sat down right there!" Connie said, pointing to the right cushion on the divan. "I read the paper as you typed. I am not dreaming this. You were upstairs thoughtfully typing. I heard you."

"Thoughtfully typing? What's that mean?" I asked.

"You know, a little at time. You weren't typing nonstop like you usually do. You'd type a short burst. Then a little more a few moments later. Sounded like you were thinking through something, maybe your thoughts about our conversation with the Tuckers. That's why I didn't bother you."

"Nope. It wasn't me," I said as I looked toward the door to the upper room staircase. Connie's eyes followed mine.

"I'd better go up," I said.

"Not yet!" Connie said, as she walked across the room and picked up the fireplace poker. "Here, take this."

I took a breath, grasped the staircase doorknob, and turned it slowly. The door opened easily and without a sound. I'd crept up and down those creaky stairs many times late at night, trying not to wake Connie. There was no way we could ascend the stairs without warning our intruder. I turned on the light, lowered my voice and yelled, "Hey! Who's up there? Anybody up there? We're coming up and we're armed." There was no response. I turned and raised my left palm toward Connie, signaling her not to follow. She nodded.

The upper room door opened inward and didn't lock. I charged up eight creaking steps, across the short landing, and burst through the door in a single uninterrupted rush of adrenaline. The room was empty. Nothing moved except the dust motes in the afternoon sun. I hooked the door with the poker and swung it away from the wall. No one was behind it. I scanned the room. My Underwood sat on the desk where it belonged. My chair was in its place, tucked neatly in the knee-hole of the desk. Textbooks, notebooks, and an unopened ream of typing paper were as I had left them. The desk light was off. Though I didn't need it, I turned it on, thinking it might reveal some hidden clue. Nothing seemed out of place.

"Connie, come on up. There's nobody here," I yelled. She joined me, and we stood in the middle of the small room and stared at each other and then surveyed the room for anything I might have missed. I sat at the desk and examined the typewriter. There was no indication someone had typed without paper. The roller was clean. The ribbon was so used it was impossible to tell a new strike from an old one.

"Someone is messing with us," I said.

"Someone or some *thing*," Connie said. "Ron, call them now, or I will."

"Okay, we'll go down together. I'll call them."

We walked down the creaking staircase into our living room. I replaced the poker and went straight for the telephone. The Tuckers were willing to talk with us right away.

"I feel awkward about this," I said before we rang the bell. "You take the lead. Okay?"

"Coward," Connie answered, but she smiled when she said it. "Okay. I don't mind. It's simple. Is the house haunted or not?" Connie rang the bell.

Mrs. Tucker came to the door. "Hello, please come in. We've been wanting to get to know you better, and we're just settling in for our afternoon cocktail. We'd love to have you join us. Tuck likes martinis. I like gimlets. How about you?"

"Oh my, no thank you," Connie said. "We don't want to bother you."

"Nothing like inviting ourselves over for a drink," I said as I laughed, thinking an afternoon cocktail was a very good idea under the circumstance. "I'll have a martini. Vodka, if you have it."

"Gin will have to do, Mr. McCall. Rocks or up?" Mrs. Tucker answered.

"Gin's fine. Rocks, please."

"Great. Let me introduce you to Tuck." She walked to the wide, arched living room entrance and allowed us to enter first. "Tuck, Mr. and Mrs. McCall are here. Isn't it nice to have someone join us for cocktails?"

Mr. Tucker stood from his wingback chair, which sat in front of a fireplace much larger than our own. A framed print of Salvador Dali's *Last Supper*, with its hovering image of a headless Jesus, hung over the mantel. Dali's surrealism was markedly incompatible with the antique furniture in the room. The adjoining bookcase was neatly organized with books, family photos and a small collection of polished geodes and crystals.

A Persian rug and evenly spaced occasional chairs defined our meeting space. Mr. Tucker smiled warmly, and slowly waved his large hand toward the chairs nearest the fireplace, inviting us to sit.

"I'm off to get the drinks. Mrs. McCall, are you sure I can't get you something?"

"Oh, no thank you, and please call me Connie."

"I'll be right back. And don't you dare start telling any ghost stories until I get back," Mrs. Tucker said. She vanished down the hall, fully aware she had just fired a supernatural warning shot across our bow.

"Yes, dear. We'll wait," her husband responded. He turned his attention back to us. "We'd better wait for Margarite if we want to keep the peace. So, how do like your new neighborhood, Mr. McCall?"

"Please, call me Ron."

"Fine, most people call me Tuck. You can too. Real name's Terrance."

"Well, Tuck, we like the neighborhood. We did have an unfortunate introduction to our neighbor, Lawrence. I assume you know what happened to him?"

"Yes, I heard what happened. Also heard you were the one who found him. Must have surprised you."

"It did. Who in the world would be cowardly enough to rob a man like Lawrence?"

"Frankly, I'm surprised it didn't happen sooner. Lawrence is dangerously consistent. Hell, you can set your watch by him. He's in front of our house at five after eight every morning. He hits the drug store by eight-fifteen, and then off to the retard's workshop five minutes later. I know how important routine is to those people, but you'd think someone would tell them to change things up a bit, just to be safe."

Connie and I both winced while he was talking. I asked, "Workshop? What kind of workshop?"

"Sorry, I didn't mean to offend. It's called the Helping Hands Workshop. It's a place where slow-thinking folks like Lawrence can go to feel useful. And, they are, I guess. Whole crew of 'em file in there every day to do piece work for local companies. You know, like putting labels on candles and stringing beads. That sort of stuff. It's in the basement of an old Catholic church just a few blocks from here. Ask me, his broken leg could have been avoided if he had just arrived late a couple of times."

"When we talked with the detective," Connie broke in, "he said that sort of thing doesn't happen very often in this neighborhood. Was he right?"

"From his perspective, I suppose he is. Margarite and I have lived here for over thirty years. I can count the number of times I've called the police on one hand, but I remember every damned one of them. So, from your cop's point of view, this is a low-crime area. From my point of view, well, let's just say I try to stay aware of what's going on around me."

"Here we are," Mrs. Tucker announced, as she entered the room with four drinks on a low-rimmed pewter tray. "A martini for you, Ron, and a glass of ice water for you, Connie, just in case you need to wet your whistle. A straight-up martini with two olives for Tuck, and a gimlet for me."

"So," Tuck said. "How can we help you?"

"Looks like we picked the right time to come, didn't we? Thank you for the refreshments. Totally unexpected," I said, attempting to ease into the conversation.

Connie wasn't interested in a slow entry. "Have you or have any of your previous tenants had paranormal experiences in this house?"

Margarite looked at Tuck, who smiled and asked, "You've been talking with Batty Matty, haven't you?"

"You mean the drugstore's Matty?"

"The same."

"What's she have to do with this?"

"Nothing, except a nose she can't keep out of everyone's business."

Connie circled back to her original question, "So, you have some ghost stories to tell us?"

"What he's trying to say," Margarite said, "Is we've heard some stories and many times Matty's name comes up in the telling."

"What kind of stories? Give me an example," Connie said.

"We hesitate to repeat them because we don't believe them," Margarite explained.

"Margarite, I can call you Margarite?" I interrupted.

"Of course."

"We didn't come down here to interrogate you. We've had several unexplainable experiences and just wanted to talk to you about them," I said.

"Well, talk, and I'll bet you a dime to a dollar, Batty Matty is tangled up in them somewhere," Tuck said. Not menacing, just confident, he reminded me of my favorite uncle, who was a master of dismissive nicknames and critical opinions. I sort of liked him.

"Tangled up. That's a little strong, maybe," Connie said. "I'll admit, she was first to suggest my concern might be the result of living in this house."

"And what was your concern?"

Connie told them the story of her failed inhaler. As she told it, her manner softened, recalling her own doubts about Matty's unsolicited comment. "Yes, I thought it was an odd thing for her to say, and I dismissed it until two other odd things occurred. Someone or something hid our TV remote control in our silverware drawer, and someone or something has been typing on Ron's typewriter in the upper room!"

"I use your little attic bedroom as a study room," I explained. "It's perfect. I have my old, manual typewriter placed on the desk in front of the window. I wasn't home, and Connie heard someone typing in the upper room for quite a long time."

Connie filled in the blanks, giving the Tuckers a play-by-play of the missing remote control and the uninvited typist. Her explanation of our trip up the creaky stairs and our fruitless investigation of the room, while armed with a fireplace poker, gave me an unnoticeable shiver.

Tuck and Margarite's eyes met in stone-faced silence. Finally, Tuck spoke, "Sure you didn't sit down to read the paper and take a little cat nap? Could have dreamed it, you know."

"It was not a dream." Connie's response was quick and certain.

"The power of suggestion is a mighty thing. Maybe Batty Matty planted a seed that took root quickly," Tuck said. "That can happen to anybody."

"Trust me, Mr. Tucker. It wasn't a dream, and I am not a person who drifts into supernatural musings at the drop of a hat. Obviously, you've had other tenants who've had similar experiences. Tell us about them. Tell us about the history of the house. We'd just like to know what's going on."

When she called him "Mr. Tucker," I knew she had shifted into high gear, and convincing her to downshift would be difficult. I said nothing and waited for a response.

"First of all, please understand there's nothing to worry about," Margarite said. "Yes, there have been other reports. The first one was shortly after we converted the upstairs to a separate apartment. We'd lived here almost ten years before we did that. Seems like as soon as we converted the place people started worrying about Rebekah Cooperman."

"Who is Rebekah Cooperman?" Connie asked.

"You mean who was Rebekah Cooperman," Tuck said. He hesitated long enough to finger boost one of his olives up the side of his martini glass. He sucked out the pimento, popped the hollow olive in his mouth, and chewed. Still chewing, he said, "She was the first wife of Simon Cooperman, who was the son of the founder of Cooperman's Department Store. Simon and his wife, Rebekah, lived here. In 1941, she was found dead in the basement with a crushed skull and a rock in her apron pocket. She was only thirty-two years old. What happened to her? Nobody knows."

"How awful. Did you know before you bought the house?" Connie asked.

"Yes, we did." Margarite said. "The realtor showed us a clipping from the *Denver Post*. He felt we should know about it before we bought the house. I mean people die in their homes all the time. We loved the place, and Rebekah Cooperman's untimely death wasn't a reason to walk away. We're glad we didn't. We still love this place."

"Rock in her pocket? That's odd," I said.

"It was a geode. Like those up there," Tuck said, pointing to his collection of polished crystal-centered stones. I knew nothing about them until I heard her story. Oddly enough, she's the reason I became a collector."

I pretended I had just noticed them. I stood and stepped closer to the bookcase to inspect the geodes.

"Wow, that's a nice collection. May I look closer? The big one on the end is a beauty. Where did you find it?" It was a baseball-sized geode, sliced in half and polished, revealing a beautiful orange, opal, and purple crystal surprise.

"That one came from Brazil. I was in the import business, which took me all over the world. While there, I went on a geode hunt. Found that baby and had it cut and polished. Isn't it something?"

"Never seen anything like it." I immediately looked past the crystal-centered rock to the family photos. One caught my eye. A much younger Tuck and Margarite accompanied by a young boy posed for a shot in a mountain campground. "Oh, is that your son," I asked.

"Yes, that's Reginald," Tuck answered. "Or, I should say, that's Reggie when he was our son. Haven't seen him in years."

"No kidding," I said, letting Tuck's response float unattended. We were trying to catch a ghost, not visit the messiness of a dysfunctional family. I returned to my seat and to my geode conversation.

"Your geodes, do you use them or just look at them?"

"You sound like you know something of their metaphysical properties," Tuck said, without answering my question.

"My Aunt Betty used 'em. Said they connected her to divine beings and helped her make better decisions. My dad thought she was crazy. He'd say, 'She's nuts. Nuts in a barrel. Doesn't keep me from loving her. But she's nuts in a barrel.'"

Connie got us back on track. "Seems like Rebekah Cooperman must have rubbed her geode the wrong way."

"Sure does," said Tuck.

"So, your very first renter was visited by Rebekah?" Connie asked.

"No, it was the second, I think," Margarite said. "She said she'd heard tapping noises in her bedroom wall, and when she learned Rebekah died in this house, she moved. Didn't even stop to get her rental deposit. She was here one day and gone the next.

"Next renter gave us another crazy report. Lady with her son lived up there for about two years. Her son slept upstairs in your study room. She claimed some of her son's favorite toys had gone missing and someone was opening his windows and turning off the night-light. Her son couldn't sleep without a night-light. She'd tuck him in, turn on the light, go back downstairs. Sometimes in the morning the window was open, and the light was turned off."

"Yeah, she was a dingbat," Tuck said. "She'd talk your head off. I have no doubt she talked to Matty about her poltergeist. She was drifty as hell. You know, just the kind of person who hears a ghost story and turns every little thing into paranormal gossip. And her son, he was just about one intellectual rung above Lawrence and not half as sweet. Probably lost his toys when he was sneaking out the window late at night. Besides, what would a damned ghost want with a bunch of toys?"

"You actually think a young kid was sneaking out of the upper room window?" I asked.

"Long way up there, I know. But it's easier to believe than some damned ghost story. Christ, you misplace your car keys, and someone will make a ghost story out of it, especially that dingbat."

"Tuck used to tell people we had a dingbat in our belfry," Margarite said with a childish giggle. Her head turned abruptly to the right in three short twitches, like someone had given her ear lobe three quick yanks.

"We were glad when they moved," Tuck said. "Lawrence missed them though, especially the boy. Lawrence used to come over and play with him all the time. They were about the same age and seemed to have a lot in common. What was the kid's name?"

"Walter. His mom called him Wally," Margarite answered. "Wally, oh Wally, where have your toys gone?" She giggled again.

"That's right, Wally. After they moved, Lawrence was sort of lost. He'd come over here out of habit. When I could, I'd sit on our front porch with him and talk a little.

"Then there was this guy named Mort Simmons," Tuck continued. "And he was a doozy. I remember because I had just returned from Haiti and all that vodou chicken-blood nonsense they want you to believe. One night Mort came to our door with alcohol on his breath, saying he was visited by a seductive female ghost. He told us he was sitting near the little fireplace reading when he saw a woman's form inside a shimmering orb of light. She stood at the door of the attic stairway and beckoned him to follow her upstairs. He was totally unnerved and moved three days later.

"I think the spook's name must have been Jack Daniels, not Rebekah Cooperman. He claimed to be an accountant, something we doubted because he was always late with his rent. No question, he had a drinking problem. He hung out with that pharmacist guy sometimes. What's his name?"

"Do you mean Ralph, Glazier's pharmacist?" Connie asked.

"Ralph. That's right. Ralph. Don't get me started on that guy."

"No. Please don't start on Ralph, dear." Margarite said. She giggled and twitched. "Just know, there's nothing to worry about," Margarite added. "There have been a couple of others, all just as hard to swallow. No, there's nothing to worry about," she repeated, as she scooted toward the front edge of her chair. It was clear the cocktail hour was about over.

I followed her lead and stood. "Well, we've taken enough of your time. Thanks very much for the cocktail. Margarite you make a mean martini. And thanks for hearing us out. We feel much better. But, if someone starts banging on my Underwood tonight, we'll come get you. Okay?"

Margarite stood. "Be sure you do," she said. Tuck just sat and raised his empty glass in a mock toast as we left the room with Margarite trailing us to the outside door. We returned to our apartment in silence. Connie brewed tea as we sat at our small kitchen table.

"Did we learn anything?" I asked.

"They are 'nuts in a barrel' to coin a phrase. And how did you come up with that stuff about your Aunt Betty? I've only met her twice, but she was very easy to be around. She was just plain sweet."

"Oh, yes she is. She also chases butterflies in January. She's more than a little flaky. And I don't think Tuck and Margarite are far behind her. Let them slurp down a couple of Margarite's drinks and spend a moment of inebriated meditation before Tuck's geodes, and they'd probably make Timothy Leary look like a schoolboy."

Connie walked to the stove to replenish her tea. "More tea?" she asked.

"No. I'm good."

"Tuck sure isn't a friend of Matty's," Connie said, as she topped off her cup and returned to the table. "And what's he got against Ralph? And Rebekah Cooperman? Now there's a story."

"And the remark he made about his son was curious. When he first said it, I was unsure how to respond, so I didn't," I explained. "Later, I toyed with the idea of probing a little, but Margarite sort of cut the meeting short."

"Gee, we better ask Batty Matty. She'll know. Damn it, we just took a deep dive into a cesspool of neighborhood gossip, but we didn't come close to answering the question about our upper-room typist. Who in the hell was up there?" Connie asked.

"I know. I know. I just can't get past Margarite telling us there's nothing to worry about. She said it three times. They both know more than they let on."

"Did you notice her tics?"

"How could you miss them? Got worse as the night went on. Don't know if it was the booze or the conversation that set her off. Are you up for sleeping here tonight?" I asked.

"Yep. Where else we going to go? Besides, I'm more curious than I am frightened. We can't leave now. I think we should take our neighbor's advice and stay fearless and enjoy the neighborhood."

Duck Boots

4

W E AWOKE EARLY AND remarkably refreshed the next morning. Connie left for work, and I had work to do upstairs but took extra time to drink my coffee before I climbed the creaky stairs. The phone rang before I could do so. It was Lawrence's mother.

"Hello, Mrs. Stroud. How are you, and how is Lawrence?"

"Well, Lawrence is fine, hobbling round, but fine. Me, well I'm a little under the weather this morning. That's why I'm calling. Lawrence been dying to return to the Helping Hands Workshop. He hasn't been there for nearly three weeks. I told him I'd take him this morning, but I can't. I was wondering if you could drop him off. He's in a walking cast, so he's fairly mobile but it's too far for him to walk."

"Sure. I can do that. Where exactly is the workshop?"

"Just drive half a block past Glazier's Pharmacy. Turn left, that'll be Grant Street. Drive two blocks south and you're there. It's an old Catholic church. Go around to the side entrance, then to the basement. Lawrence will show you."

"When's he need to be there?"

"He's usually there by twenty after eight. But whenever it's most convenient for you. Don't worry about bringing him home. Someone there will do it."

I glanced at my watch. "I'll come over right now. I'm just starting my day and moving around a little will be a great wake up."

"Thank you, thank you, Ron. You're a life saver, and Lawrence will be glad to see you."

"It's really no problem at all. And it'll be great to see him. We've missed him. Have they made any progress on catching the guy who robbed him?"

"We haven't heard a thing."

"Takes time, I guess. I'll be right over."

Our parking spots were just off the alley behind the house and alongside the Tucker's freestanding garage. I circled the block to be on the right side of the street to pick up Lawrence. As soon as I rang the bell and Mrs. Stroud opened the door, I heard Lawrence chant my new name, "Coop, Coop, Coop."

Once in the car, Lawrence was quiet, even with my prompting. "How you feeling, Lawrence?" I asked.

"Good, good," he answered.

"Cast looks kinda heavy. Is it?"

"Yeah, yeah, kinda heavy."

As we drove past our apartment, I took a chance. "Bells and chimes are going to ring," I said. His answer was immediate, "Mamie Eisenhower, Mamie Eisenhower, Mamie Eisenhower." He looked straight ahead as he said it, but I thought I noticed a fleeting smile on his face when he finished the refrain.

"I'll bet it will feel good to get back to work."

"Good," he said. "See Sam. Friend, friend, friend."

It was a short ride. Lawrence led me to a side door of the church and down a short flight of stairs, which he limped down without too much difficulty. As soon as we entered the room, we were greeted by a tall, bearded man with a welcoming smile. His teeth flashed white against the solid black of his bushy beard. It was the first thing you noticed. The second thing was his velvety baritone voice. He was a model father figure.

Without touching Lawrence, he raised his arms in a grand welcome home gesture and presented him to the scattered assemblage of Helping Hands workers who sat at six long, well-organized tables full of empty first-aid boxes and assorted first-aid materials.

"Hey, everybody! Look who's here," Sam announced. Then he began to clap, and his twenty-person audience joined him with a heartfelt round of applause, accompanied by smiles, hoots, and table thumps. Lawrence raised his right hand in a quick, self-conscience wave and began to limp down the row of tables.

"Lawrence, why don't you sit toward the front today. It'll save you a few steps," the man said, pulling a chair out for Lawrence, who dutifully sat. Then the man turned to me and extended his hand.

"Hello, I'm Sam Richards. You must be Mr. McCall. Lawrence's mom called. She told me you'd be bringing him over this morning. Thank you."

Lawrence heard the introduction and corrected his manager, "Coop, Coop, Coop," he said.

"That's what Lawrence calls me because of where we live. We live in the Cooperman House," I said. "Sam, nice meeting you. First name's Ron. This is quite an operation. Looks like there's a day's work ahead of you. I'll let you get to it. Mrs. Stroud said someone else would take him home. Is that right?"

"Yep, we have him covered. Say, do you have two seconds to talk? We have some more folks coming, so I can't start the assembly ball rolling just yet."

"Sure."

Sam walked me out of the workroom to the foot of the basement stairs.

"I couldn't believe it when I heard what happened. Have you heard anything about who attacked him?" Sam asked.

"I haven't heard a word."

"The police came by to talk to me, but I'm afraid I wasn't much help. Everybody loves Lawrence," Sam said.

"They talked to me too. I didn't help them much, either, and I'm the guy who found him lying in the snow."

"Really. That must've been a shocker."

"Yes, it was. We're new to the neighborhood. So, we really didn't know what to make of it."

"Well, it's unusual. I've had twenty-some people show up here almost every weekday for over three years. Many of them walk to get here. Never had a problem before. Just hope this one was an anomaly."

"Me too. And I hope they get the guy. It remains a mystery. Lawrence certainly didn't know who hit him. All he said about the guy was he smelled bad."

"Now, there's a lead for you. Well, welcome to the neighborhood. Sorry you had such a rough entry, but at least you've made a new friend. If Lawrence already has a nickname for you, you are his friend. How do you like the Cooperman House?"

"So far, so good," I said, waiting for the requisite paranormal question to land. It never did.

"It's a grand old house," Sam said.

"Are you familiar with it?"

"No. Not really. I drive by it often. In fact, I did yesterday when I stopped by to check on Lawrence. Cooperman House and Lawrence's house kind of make the neighborhood, don't they? Well, I won't keep you. Thanks for the word. And for delivering Lawrence. I'll bet we'll see each other again while he's recovering."

I drove home. The coffee was still hot, so I poured a cup a little too full and carefully walked up the stairs to the upper room. Like the day before, nothing was amiss. I opened the top right-hand drawer of my desk, removed a piece of paper from the depleted stack, spun it into the carriage, and reached for my notebook. Typing my notes from the previous day's classes was part of my study routine.

I sat and stared at the keyboard, hesitant to strike a key. Finally, I typed "Profiling Pitfalls, October 13, 1978, Prof. Woodside" at the top of the page. Our resident spook didn't seem to mind. Still, I chose not to type another word. If someone other than me had been typing on my Underwood, they would have left fingerprints. I'd call Sergeant Bloomfield for assistance. He hadn't returned my duck boots, which gave me a reason to call. Bloomfield answered on the second ring.

"Hello Sergeant, this is Ron McCall. Just wondered about your progress on Lawrence Stroud's case and if my duck boots helped you."

"Duck boots? Oh, crap. Please, forgive me," Bloomfield said. "I just plain forgot about them. I'll have someone bring them over this afternoon. And yes, they did help us a little. We found a full boot print and a partial that belonged to an unidentified person. Unfortunately, we have no idea who the person is. That's about all I can tell you about the case."

"You know, it'd be great if you could bring them over yourself. I have something else I'd like to talk to you about."

"I guess I could swing by this afternoon, late. What's going on?"

"Tough to explain over the phone. Can it wait until you get here?"

"Sure, I guess. Sorry about your boots. I should be over about four."

Sergeant Bloomfield didn't arrive until close to five. Connie came home about two minutes later and hurried up the back stairs, took off her jacket, and joined us in the living room. I hadn't decided how I was going to approach our paranormal suspicions with the detective. Suggesting we had a ghost was certain to make us seem weird and reduce our credibility. As it turned out, Connie's head-on manner made the decision for me.

"Connie, you remember Sergeant Bloomfield," I said. "He was kind enough to return my boots and I was about to explain some of our other concerns to him."

"Oh, you mean the ghost who's been using your typewriter?" she asked.

"Well, now, of course we don't think it's a ghost. But we've had an intruder. It's mysterious, but certainly not a ghost," I said.

"An intruder? What makes you think so?" Bloomfield said.

"Connie, tell him what happened."

Connie sat down on one end of the divan and invited Sergeant Bloomfield to sit on the other. She told the story without interruption, while I remained standing. I watched Bloomfield's face closely. He was unresponsive.

"As far as we know, ghosts don't leave fingerprints," I said. "That's why we wondered if you could have my typewriter checked for prints to give us some clue who our visitor is," I said.

"No need for that," Bloomfield said. "Must be Rebekah."

"What? What did you say?" Connie gasped.

"You mean Rebekah Cooperman?" I asked.

"Yep. She's been hanging around here for years. At least, that's what people say."

"The ghost of Rebekah Cooperman is common knowledge?" Connie asked.

"Well, I wouldn't say common knowledge, but most of us on the force know about it. We've had calls over the years that seemed to lead back to Rebekah because of her unexplained death. I don't believe any of them. But you know, when a story becomes folklore, it's hard to stop. So, here we are in the Cooperman House with still another unexplained occurrence. Certainly, my job is to explain the unexplained. Rebekah's death is unexplained and may have been a crime. Your noisy typewriter is unexplained. Unfortunately, it is not yet a crime. That makes helping you with fingerprints difficult."

"But not impossible?" Connie asked.

Bloomfield studied Connie for a moment. Then looked at me and smiled. We seemed to have developed a connection. It wasn't friendship; it was more like measured appreciation. It could have been because we shared a professional path or because we both were authentically concerned about Lawrence. Whatever the reason, he was willing to help.

"Well, I suppose not. All you want to do is look for foreign prints on the typewriter, right. Sort of like my process of elimination with your boot prints, right? I can probably get you that far but comparing fingerprints against a government database won't be possible."

"Okay. How do we do that?" I asked.

"First, you must understand this is not official police business. I'll ask my favorite lab technician if she's up for a little moonlighting. If she is, she'll call you. Won't cost much. Maybe forty bucks or so. But it isn't police business just yet. Until it is, the results can't be used in court and, of course, you'll both need to agree to be fingerprinted. And my tech? You never met her."

"Have her call us," I said, then looked at Connie for approval. She nodded.

"Her name is Lori Crawford. I think she'll want to do it. She loves this kind of stuff."

"Sooner the better. I need to use the typewriter," I said.

Lori Crawford called the next morning and came over the same evening. She was a short, physically fit woman with closely cropped hair and active brown eyes. She was pleasant, but businesslike, and held tight to the handle of a worn, brown attaché case with her left hand. She looked like a cop. She talked like a sailor. "Nice meeting you both," she said. "Where's the spooky badass typewriter?"

"It's upstairs. I've barely touched it since the incident."

"Tell me more about the incident."

I explained what happened, emphasizing we didn't believe in ghosts, even though there were people who did because of the history of the house. "Are you familiar with the Rebekah Cooperman story?"

"Oh, no shit. This is the Cooperman House? My sister's into all that supernatural crap. She's mentioned Rebekah a couple of times. This is great. If I can help debunk one of her paranormal bullshit stories, I would love it. Lead me to the typewriter."

I led our fingerprint expert to the upper room. She sat at the desk and went to work. "This'll take me twenty minutes or so. You can watch me or wait downstairs for me to finish. It's up to you."

"I'll leave you to it. Can I get you anything? Soda, tea, water?"

"I'm good. I'll have my hands full here. I'll be down and take your prints when I'm through here."

I joined Connie in the living room. "Well, how are you betting? Will she find something or not?" I asked.

Connie smiled and mimicked Margarite's head twitch. "Ghosts don't leave fingerprints. There's nothing to worry about," she teased.

I smiled back and said, "Batty Matty would love this, wouldn't she?"

Lori was finished in fifteen minutes and came down the stairs smiling. "There were prints. Most of them were on the body of the machine, not on the keys. I suspect they are yours, Ron. I doubt that I'll need to take your prints. But I have a question for you. Have you ever worn rubber gloves when you typed?"

"No. Can't imagine why I would."

"Me neither. That's why I was surprised to find this." Lori held up a small paper envelope, cupped it open and emptied a tiny, white sliver of rubber into my palm. "Looks like your ghost wears rubber gloves when he types. Wonder if he still uses a condom?"

Connie laughed, but was quick to get back to business. "Sure our ghost's a he, are you?"

"No, of course not. The only thing I'm sure of is somebody, some living, breathing soul was typing on your typewriter that day."

"Where exactly did you find it?" I asked.

"It was wedged, out of sight, just beneath the right edge of the space bar. My guess is a little flap of rubber got caught beneath the space bar and the body of the machine. The typist's hand was probably pulled back quick, leaving this behind. Hardly enough to notice if you are thinking hard and typing fast."

"Wow. That's amazing. A little piece of rubber. That's worth every penny," I said and handed her the check we had already prepared. "Thank you, Lori."

"And thank you. I can't wait to talk to my sister."

Sniff Test

5

OVER THE NEXT TWO weeks I took Lawrence to the workshop three times. We were becoming friends in a special uncluttered way. Normal give-and-take conversation was beyond us, and I came to realize being glad to see one another was enough.

"Lawrence, good morning," I said, as his mother walked him to my car. I opened the door for him and helped him sit slowly and swing his casted leg inside the car.

"Coop, Coop, Coop," he said.

"You ready to go to work?"

"Work, work, work. Sam, Sam, Sam."

I shut the car door and spoke to his mother, "He still has a ride home, right? I'm open if you need me. My afternoon class has been cancelled."

"We're covered, Ron. Thank you so much for your help."

Lawrence and I walked down the basement stairs at Helping Hands right on time. I stuck my head in the door just far enough to wave at Sam and noted his eager workers were about to assemble small bottles of shampoo, conditioner, and hand cream for a regional hotel group. Sam acknowledged with an index finger held high. He wanted a word with me.

"Hey, Ron. I wanted to revisit something you said. Lawrence said his attacker smelled bad. Is that right?"

"Yes. He repeated it several times."

"What did he mean? Did he mean body odor?

"I don't know."

"Could it have been a chemical smell of some kind?"

"I suppose. Why? What's on your mind?"

"We have a new guest this morning. He came in on his own and seemed not to be a person with special needs. And he smells like ammonia. He's standing by the coffee pot, drinking coffee."

I casually glanced his way. The hatless man with matted black hair wore a soiled Carhartt barn jacket over a black logoed hooded sweatshirt. The filthy jacket concealed most of the sweatshirt logo, so it was not legible. "Did he wear a Broncos stocking cap?" I asked.

"I don't know. I didn't see him come in."

"Do you often have street people stop in to get warm and have a cup of coffee?"

"From time to time. They're welcome to the coffee. But I explain the work we do, and they usually move along. I haven't spoken to this guy, mostly because of his overpowering odor. I went over to talk to him but smelled the ammonia, poured a cup of coffee, and walked away. Do you think we should talk to someone about it? I know it could be nothing, but you never know."

"I think we should call Sergeant Bloomfield. He's the detective working the case. I've got his business card in my wallet. Do you have a private phone handy?"

"Got a phone, but it isn't private. It's on my desk by the back wall, plenty far away from Mr. Stink. I think you could talk without him hearing."

With that he stepped farther inside the room and pointed toward his desk. I waved my thanks and went straight to the phone. I was surprised when Sergeant Bloomfield answered. "Hello, Sergeant. This is Ron McCall. I hope you are free to talk. I have a lead you may want to check."

"Speak to me, Ron. I'm all ears."

I explained our ammonia-saturated visitor and our unfounded suspicions. I also explained that Sam was the man in charge, and I would probably need to leave to avoid setting off any alarms.

"Can Sam keep him there?"

"I don't know. Under normal circumstances, they would encourage him to leave."

"Tell you what. You go ahead and leave the building, but not the grounds. Are you parked where you can see the exit door?"

"Yes, illegally. I was just dropping off Lawrence."

"Just sit in the car for a while and watch. I can be there in twenty minutes. If he leaves and walks away, watch where he goes. If he gets in a car, get the plate number if you can. But don't follow him. Just hang out. Don't follow him. Okay?" Bloomfield said.

I hung up, turned toward Sam, and gave him a right-handed okay sign and a huge smile. As far as anyone in the room knew, whatever we were concerned about before the call had turned out just fine. I rejoined Sam at the end of the room.

"Bloomfield will be here in twenty minutes. If you can, let the guy hang around a while. You know, just don't ask him to leave unless you absolutely must. If he leaves, that's okay. I'll be outside watching. One other thing, if you can, keep him away from Lawrence. There's no telling what Lawrence would do if he recognized the smell of his assailant. I don't think he'd be quiet about it."

"Right, but Lawrence's nose could be the answer," Sam said.

"Yes, it might be. Eventually, we'll give him a whiff of ammonia and see what he says. Involving Lawrence in an undercover sniff test on the guy isn't a good idea. I'm leaving. I'll be right outside in my car."

I'd parked in a no-parking zone designed to keep the pedestrian crosswalk clear. Moving the car to an open spot along the curb on the opposite side of the street made sense. I'd be less obvious and have a better view of the door to the basement staircase. Fifteen minutes later, our suspect exited the basement door and walked half a block east up the one-way street. He was wearing a Broncos stocking cap. He crossed the street and unlocked the door of a well-used, black Jeep Cherokee, which sat three cars in front of me. I couldn't see the license plate from where I sat. He started the car but didn't pull away from the curb immediately. While I waited, Sergeant Bloomfield parked in the no-parking zone I had previously occupied.

He walked toward the basement stairs. I took a chance and sounded the car horn with two short beeps. He turned and looked. I motioned toward the Jeep with an emphatic index finger. Bloomfield had no idea our suspect was seated in a Jeep three cars in front of me. After glancing down the street, he waved big and said, "Hey Ron. How you doing? Long time no see," and walked across the street to my open window.

"He is in the black Jeep about three cars up. I couldn't get the plates."

"I see it. Why don't we take a little ride together? Scoot over. I'm driving."

I did as he said. The bench seat in my '72 Chevy Bel Air made it easy.

"If he pulls out, that's fine. But he doesn't need to for us to get his number. The car behind him isn't parked close. We'll just drive by, and you and your young eyes can get the number."

We drove by slowly. I got the plate number and paid no attention to the suspect. "Colorado BA882," I said, as I wrote it down on the small notepad he'd given me.

"Good. That's about all we can do for now. He's broken no laws. There's no reason to approach him. We'll go around the block and go see Sam. That's right, isn't it? Sam?"

"That's right. No need to make sure he doesn't see us?"

"Nah. We got what we need. Plus, he could just as easily see us sneaking around. Act normal and we will seem normal." Once back inside, I introduced Bloomfield to Sam.

"How'd you guys do out there?" Sam asked. "I put the group to work and was about to go chat with the guy when he left. Finished his coffee and left."

"We got the plate number," I said.

"Think you could identify his coffee cup?" asked Bloomfield.

"Geeze, I doubt it. Trash can's full of them. But I've found something for our sniff test."

"Sniff test?" asked Bloomfield.

"Yeah. Lawrence said his attacker smelled bad. Lawrence forgets nothing. If he smells ammonia, he'll be able to tell us if it is the same odor carried by his attacker." Sam handed me a jug of ammonia-based cleaning fluid. I popped the cap and sniffed.

"Yep. That should do it," I said as I quickly moved the jug away from my nose and handed it to Bloomfield. "How should we handle this? Should we explain to Lawrence what we're up to or just expose him to it and wait for a response?"

"Let me do this. I think it would be better to remind him of the attack and then casually introduce him to the smell," Bloomfield said.

"Okay. It's about break time. I'll stop the assembly line and we can talk with him."

The Helping Hand workers put down their boxes and bottles. It was a restroom break and there was a table of chilled soft drinks, coffee, and cake donuts. Lawrence turned from his table and swung his casted leg toward us. That's when he saw me.

"Coop, Coop, Coop," he said.

"Hey, Lawrence. There's someone here who wants to meet you."

"Meet me. Meet me."

"Yes. This is Sergeant Bloomfield. He's a policeman."

"Lawrence, it's nice to meet you. I understand your dad was a policeman."

"Dad a policeman."

"I didn't know him, but I know about him. Many people loved him, and he was a very brave man."

"Bells and chimes are going to ring. Mamie Eisenhower, Mamie Eisenhower, Mamie Eisenhower."

I joined Lawrence in his vocal tribute to his father, softly repeating Mamie Eisenhower's name as he chanted. This was new territory for Bloomfield. He took it in stride.

"Lawrence, I've been trying to figure out who hurt you that day in the snow. Will you do me a favor?" Bloomfield asked.

"Favor, favor, favor," Lawrence said.

"Great. Thank you. All I want you to do is smell this bottle," Bloomfield said.

He removed the cap from the cleaning-fluid jug and handed it to Lawrence. Lawrence put it to his nose and turn away quickly. He sniffed again. His response was emphatic, "Man smell bad. Man smell bad. Hit me. Hit me. Hit me. Smell bad."

"The man who hit you smelled like this?" Bloomfield asked.

"Yes. Smell bad," Lawrence nodded vigorously. "Man smell bad."

"Thank you, Lawrence. You have been a big help," Bloomfield said.

"Lawrence, we are taking up most of your breaktime. Can I help you to the bathroom?" Sam asked.

"I go, I go, I go," Lawrence said. He rose and limped to the restroom on his walking cast.

"Well, I've got some work to do," Bloomfield said. "Thank you, gentlemen. You're great detectives. I'll let you know what I learn. And remember, loose lips sink ships. Please keep our success this morning to yourselves. You'd be amazed how a little innocent gossip can foul things up." He hurried up the basement stairs to his car.

"Well, Sam, don't you just love it when hunches become truth? Thank you."

"Doesn't happen often but looks like it might have today."

"I'll bet Bloomfield will be all over this like a dirty shirt. If he calls me, I'll let you know what he says. We should trade phone numbers."

He gave me a business card. I asked for another and wrote my number on the back of it as Lawrence made his way back from the restroom with a quick stop at the snack table. He grabbed a cake donut and returned to his seat.

"Lawrence, I'm going to take off now. Your mom asked me to bring you over tomorrow morning too. I'll see you then."

"Coop, Coop, Coop," Lawrence responded.

Rebekah's Rebuke

6

I WAS ALREADY LATE FOR my class. It would take another thirty minutes to get there and get parked, so I blew it off altogether. I was still pumped by our successful detective work. It may have been a weak lead, but it was something.

I went home and worked on a term paper for another class as I waited to tell Connie of our success. To my mind, she was exempt from Bloomfield's demand for secrecy. She'd want to know how someone acquires the smell of ammonia. I couldn't help speculating. Did our suspect work in a place where ammonia was prominent? Did he make a habit of washing his clothes in floor cleaner? Was he forced to take shelter in an unsafe area, an area permeated with ammonia? After I told her the story, Connie had an idea of her own.

"My Great Aunt Anna had ammonia breath," Connie said.

"Ammonia breath? What the hell is that?" I asked.

"It happens sometimes when you have kidney problems. If your kidneys don't clean the bad stuff from your blood, it stays with you. It can make your breath smell like ammonia. Aunt Anna finally got the problem solved, but there was a time when my dad retreated to the backyard or his workshop every time she came over. He couldn't stand it. He called her Anhydrous Annie."

"Really, is that a true story?" I asked.

"Cross my heart."

"That's an option even Bloomfield couldn't come up with."

"You had quite a day, didn't you? Were you nervous?"

"Surprisingly not. But I will admit, I was very relieved when Bloomfield arrived. Sam and I were just winging it, you know. You'll have to meet him. He is a great guy. I wonder if he's feeling as tired as I am, right now."

Connie said, "He sounds interesting. What's even more interesting, even amazing, is how we've become knee-deep in neighborhood problems in such a short period. I mean, we've covered a lot of ground. New school, new town, new job. And, as if that wasn't enough, we must solve crimes and chase ghosts."

"Yeah. This house has given us quite a ride, hasn't it? Have you talked to anybody at work about it?"

"I've made friends, but I'm not about to tell them we think our apartment is haunted. I've mentioned the attack on Lawrence a couple of times, but I won't tell anyone we are hunting a criminal with ammonia breath."

The phone interrupted our conversation.

"Ron, this is Bloomfield. Just wanted you to know the license plate number gave us a name, and the name gave us an address. Could be an empty lot, but we're headed there as soon as I put the phone down."

"Tremendous! Who the hell is he?"

"Can't say, right now. Remember, keep this all under your hat until we know more. In particular, don't talk to Lawrence's mother. Not Matty. Not even Sam, if you can help it. Got it?"

"Got it."

"Talk soon. Goodbye."

"That was Bloomfield. They have a name and address of the guy, which he wouldn't share. He reminded me again to remain mum. I don't know who we'd talk to. Shouldn't be hard to stay quiet, although I told Sam I'd call him. I guess that can wait until we know more."

"Not even your partner in crime, Matty?"

"Especially not her, and not Helen Stroud either. Bloomfield mentioned them by name."

"I suppose it makes sense," Connie said. "Well, it was good of him to call you. He must see you as part of the team."

"I doubt that, though we did seem to hit it off during the stinky-man probe at Helping Hands. But I think his easygoing manner is just a way to make people relax around his authority. It seems to work. Plus, if he's paying special attention to this case, it isn't about me. It's more about his protective affection for Lawrence because his dad was a cop. If he sees me as part of this team, I'm more than happy to ride the bench. I wonder if Professor Woodside would be proud of me."

"Remind me. Who is he?"

"I'm taking his course in criminal profiling. He's also my advisor, and I have my first meeting with him this Friday. He's ex-FBI. Think I should mention any of this? Of course, I wouldn't wade into the restricted details."

"Bloomfield just told you not to, didn't he?" Connie asked. "Though your professor may enjoy hearing about one of his students who's helping catch a criminal. It may be a breather from the refined air of academia."

"Well, he isn't a refined-air kind of guy. He looks like a drill sergeant in horn-rimmed glasses. Think Bloomfield with a graduate degree, add fifteen years with the FBI and two or three crime-stopper books and you've got Professor Woodside. Plus, he's a consultant for a lot of high-profile cases. But I think you're right. I'll do as Bloomfield asked."

On Friday afternoon I sat in a cluttered but comfortable corner office in Bennett Hall. Professor Woodside looked across his desk, smiled, and said, "Welcome, Ron. How's your first semester going?"

"Fine," I said.

"Hope so. You are one of only three full-ride graduate students. We're excited about your potential. Looks like your classwork is going well. We like to let you get your feet wet before we meet with you the first time. Looking at your schedule, I see you've opted to take more than a full load. Been busy?"

"Yes. But I want to finish in two years. I'm well organized. I'm recently married, so I won't have many social distractions. Plus, I doubt if my wife will want to be the sole provider for much longer than that."

"What's she do?"

"She teaches fourth grade at a public school. It's her first job, so we have a lot of new things going on."

"I read your application. It was well done. Still, I'd like to hear what led you in this direction. Forensic psychology is a pretty specialized field of study."

"As an undergraduate, I was all over the place. Journalism, microbiology, anthropology, and, finally, psychology. I guess the common denominator is the search. For me, finding answers to tough questions is rewarding. Even fun. I find human behavior fascinating. Why not use what you learn about it to find answers to tough questions? Too simplistic?"

"Not at all. I'd say succinct rather than simplistic. Ron, if you find yourself worrying about anything along the way, come see me. This is just a get-acquainted meeting, and it's my invitation to you to use me. Got an issue with anything, come see me."

"Thank you, Professor. I did bring you something." I reached inside my backpack and retrieved a paper prepared for his class. "This is the assignment due Monday. Is it okay if I give it to you today?"

"Sure. It'll let me get a little jump on things."

"Great, thank you." I handed him the ten-page document, bound in a blue plastic folder. He instinctively opened the folder to review the title page. He found something else. It was a single sheet of white paper with a typed message, which he read without expression. "What's this?" he asked as he handed it to me. There was a single-spaced, three-verse limerick, typed perfectly in the center of the page.

Rebekah's Rebuke

For so many years it's been said,
I died from a blow to my head.
While my heartbeat is gone,
My sad spirit lives on.
Since I'm only partially dead.

Was I laid low for vengeance or profit,
Who placed my name on death's docket?
My cranium was crushed,
My charmed life was hushed,
When I fell with a rock in my pocket.

I'm suspended betwixt and between,
There with you, but totally unseen.
My anger is swelling,
With you in my dwelling.
My response could be considered obscene.

I read the title and the first two lines, caught my breath, and tried to respond, "Oh, oh, I'm sorry," I stuttered. "I'm not sure what this is but it doesn't belong there. I certainly didn't put it there. I'm so sorry."

Professor Woodside paused, set aside my report, and said, "By the look on your face, I think it's a little more than just a misplaced piece of paper. Want to tell me about it?"

"I'm not sure you have time."

"I have twenty minutes. Talk, if you want to."

After reading the limerick through, I told him everything. I told him about the suspected paranormal behavior in the upper room and about Rebekah Cooperman and our eccentric landlords. Two mysteries folded into one, and I disobeyed Bloomfield. I told him about Lawrence and the stinky man. "And now this," I said. "I have no idea where it came from." I examined the page very closely.

"This document was typed on my typewriter. I don't know when. I don't know who typed it, and I don't know how in the hell it found its way inside my assignment cover."

"How do you know it was typed on your typewriter?"

"My typewriter has a slightly defective capital M. The vertical leg on the right side of the letter has a small void." I moved to his side of the desk to allow him to get a closer look at the imperfect M.

"Ron, you will be very good at this work. Your attention to detail is marvelous," he said as we both looked down at the mysterious page. Then he looked up at me over the top of his glasses. "But know one thing, Ron. For you and me there are no ghosts. We are not built to wallow in this mystical crap. Hear me. There are no ghosts. Ron, I really do have to wrap this up today. But come see me Monday after class. There is someone I want you to meet. Can you do that?"

"Of course," I said.

I went straight home. I couldn't wait to tell Connie about our new paranormal visit. She was due home in about an hour, and I became curiously aware of how happy I was to have her to share it with.

When she arrived, I ushered her into our living room and said, "Do I have a story to tell you!"

"A story. I can't wait," she replied as she took off her jacket, tossed in on the divan and sat beside it. I handed her the Rebekah poem.

"What's this?" she asked as she glanced at the page.

"It is a limerick, thoughtfully typed on my typewriter. It was secretly placed inside my report folder, which I gave to Professor Woodside today. Do you believe it? My first major assignment for my graduate advisor was accompanied by a paranormal poem?"

She read it. Then read it again. "This is just plain creepy. Did he see it?"

"Yep. I handed him the folder. He found the page and read it and was totally confused. Of course, no more than I was. I know it was typed on my typewriter because of the little chip in the letter M. Look closely. You'll see it."

"Well, there you have it. There are no ghosts," Connie said. "Someone, some living, breathing person wearing rubber gloves has been in the upper room playing tricks."

"You are exactly right."

"Jeez, how did you explain it all to your professor?"

"I told him the whole story, which led him to the same conclusion. There are no ghosts. In fact, I think he felt the need to prove it. He invited me to join him after class on Monday to meet someone. I have no idea who."

Duplicitous Truth

7

WHEN I ENTERED THE professor's room on Monday, he and his mystery friend stood up as Woodside said, "Ron, meet Pastor Archie Collins. He's an old friend, an ordained minister, has his own church, and he has a second calling I thought you'd find interesting. Paranormal encounters are right up his alley. Pastor, this is the grad student I told you about, Ron McCall." Woodside turned his attention to me. "I've spoken to Pastor Collins about your eventful first semester, so he knows some of your concerns. Why don't we let him begin? Please sit," he said, pointing to a strategically placed empty chair in front and to the right of his desk. The pastor sat to the left.

Pastor Collins wore khakis and a plaid open-collared shirt. He had a friendly but peculiar face. His head seemed unusually large, thanks to his flat forehead. It didn't slope. It went straight up to his distinctly black hairline. His lazy lids draped across the corner of his large eyes like a drawn-back theater curtain. His button nose sat between his large eyes and dominant chin, adding to the overall vertical appearance of his face. His toothy smile was huge, genuine, and unassuming. It wanted to sell you nothing but could probably sell you just about anything.

"Nice meeting you, Ron. There's a good deal new in your life these days, including a ghost, I understand,"

"Or something," I said, smiling.

"Can you guess what I do when I'm not bringing people to God?"

"I'd be afraid to try."

"I scare the hell out of them."

"You what?"

"I'm an entertainer, a ghost comedian, a paranormal jester."

"He has quite a following," Professor Woodside cut in. "Don't expect him to baptize you around Halloween. He'll be busy elsewhere."

"I work best in small venues, like people's homes and church conference rooms and school rooms, even some corporate settings, but seldom with more than twenty folks at a time. People hire me to scare them. People like to be frightened. I tell compelling ghost stories. Stories, I'm told, which raise the hair on the necks of even the most hard-nosed skeptics."

Without warning, a plaster vase crashed to the floor from atop Professor Woodside's seven-shelf bookcase. The gaudy, red vase exploded into a scattered mess of benign plaster shards. It startled me. Professor Woodside acted startled, and Pastor Collins just flashed a mischievous smile.

"As I tell the stories, I let special effects, like falling theater props, add to the ghostly ambiance. Sometimes people in my audience actually feel spirits touch them in a darkened room."

I felt a female presence brush my right arm and pass by me. My back straightened and I slid my elbow from the arm of the chair.

"In the right setting, a puff of perfumed air can become a spirit-filled experience."

"Professor, where was that picture taken?" the Pastor asked, pointing to a framed photo hanging behind Woodside's desk. In it, Professor Woodside was shaking hands with John F. Kennedy as a half dozen other young men in neckties and white, button-down shirts awaited their turn.

"It was taken during President Kennedy's surprise visit to my class's inaugural day in the FBI."

"A memorable day, I'm sure. I'm glad someone had a camera. One of my favorite ghostly ploys is to place attention on something present in the room with a story behind it. That photo is perfect. There the professor stands, shaking hands with our assassinated president. It's a great time to suggest violent death often contributes to souls being trapped between their old life and their final destination. Why not have the picture acknowledge that duplicitous truth?"

The framed photo tilted abruptly to the left on its hanger. I watched the picture shift, stop, and settle quietly against the wall. I had no clue how he did it.

"You see, it is all theater. I'm hired. I'm paid to entertain small groups of people by scaring them. They know it's a magic show and isn't supernatural. Still, for a diversionary moment, they allow themselves to believe ghosts are real. Professor Woodside and I hope you never do. Do you have questions?"

"About your performance? Yes. I doubt you'd answer them though. About the reality of ghosts? No. My wife and I have reached the same conclusion. There are no ghosts. The poem placed inside my report for Professor Woodside sort of sealed the deal. We've never heard of something being created by a ghost. Pictures tilt, and vases fall, but leaving a note behind breaks the rules, especially when it's typed on my typewriter. Still, when it's happening in your own home, it's hard not to get a little spooked."

"Anybody would. Even old FBI Ironsides over there," the pastor said, pointing to Professor Woodside.

"I wish my wife could have seen your performance. It was absolutely affirming. Thank you," I said.

"You're welcome. Here are my cards. One's for my spooky business. One's for my church. If you want to choose one over the other, choose the church. Sometimes, I wish it was as easy to convince people to believe in God as it is to make them believe in ghosts."

"Glad you could join us today, Ron," Professor Woodside said. "When I saw your face as I handed you the mystery poem, I thought of Pastor Collins. I've watched him frighten people many times. Then, after I heard the rest of your story, I knew you had to meet him. As you've seen, he has a few tricks up his sleeve and might be able to help you."

"Call me anytime, Ron. I don't have all the answers, but I'm in your corner. You never know, we may be able to reveal your tricky ghost with a few tricks of our own," Pastor Collins said.

"Ron, whatever happens, know that we both are interested in your next chapter," Professor Woodside said. "For now, you can take off. The pastor and I need to spend some time debugging my office. See you next Wednesday."

"Thank you. Thank you both. See you Wednesday, Professor."

———

When I pulled into my alleyway parking spot, I noticed our neighbor, Art Mingus, raking leaves in his backyard. "Hey, Art. Got a moment?"

"Sure. What's up?"

I walked to the chain-link fence that separated our yards and placed my hands on the horizontal crossbar. "Your yard looks great. Should, as hard as you work on it. How long have you lived here?"

"Long enough to know which neighbors I shouldn't let borrow my tools. Tuck's one of 'em. He's the most unhandy man I ever met. Doesn't know a screwdriver from a toothbrush. To answer your question, I been here almost twenty-five years."

"Can I ask you a strange question?"

"Strange, you say? I'm interested. Ask away."

I was not timid. I spit out the question with no sheepish smile or apologetic laugh, just a straight-forward, unfettered question. "Have you heard our house might be haunted?"

Art looked at me as if he was glad I had finally asked. "Rebekah Cooperman is dead and gone, in spite of rumors to the contrary," he said.

"I think you are absolutely right."

"But, you know, rumors are easily kept alive if you feed them occasionally. Who've you been talking to?"

"That's not important right now. I just wanted to know if the rumor had floated your way."

"Sure it has. And some people who've lived in that place have been convinced of Rebekah's presence. But it's nonsense. Ghosts don't exist. If they did, my dead wife would be all over me for giving away her stupid parakeet and not making our bed every morning."

"I'll bet she's proud of your yard though."

"She hasn't said a word about it. Don't expect she will."

"Thanks, Art." I took my hands off the fence rail and walked toward the house. Our back door was atop a flight of sturdy, wooden stairs, which zigzagged up from the backyard and around a capped chimney that protruded from the side of the house.

"Next time I see Rebekah, I'll give her your best," I yelled from the top of the stairs.

Art laughed.

The phone rang as soon as I entered our apartment.

"Hello, Ron. This is Sergeant Bloomfield. Thanks to you and Sam, we think we have the ammonia mugger. I can't give you his name because he's still just a suspect. We have him and his boots, which match the snow tracks. We understand his ammonia stench. We have his cap, which I'm sure will have a Lawrence hair or two in it. He'll be charged later today."

"That's fantastic," I said. "How'd you do it?"

"Pretty simple, really. His license plate led us to him. Went to his place, which was a trashed-out trailer in a trailer court south of town. Lucky for us, he works nights, so he was there sleeping. Came with us with no fuss whatsoever."

"Did he have ammonia breath?"

"What?"

"Never mind. Why did he smell of ammonia?"

"Works at a fertilizer plant east of Aurora. We talked to his boss. Part of his job is to bleed a small amount of pressurized anhydrous ammonia from some hoses before he leaves each morning. He's supposed to stand out of the way but apparently doesn't know upwind from downwind. Plus, from the smell of things, he doesn't change clothing very often."

"Why Lawrence? Did he say?"

"No. That's why he's still a suspect. We don't even know why he was in your neighborhood. It's a long way from his home and his job. We'll find out. For now, I wanted you to know we have a suspect in custody. And that's the word to use. He's a suspect. I've already called Lawrence's mom."

"So, we can talk about it with others."

"Sure. Sam should know. Matty too, I guess. Thank them both for me, will you?

"Thank you for filling me in, Sergeant. Much appreciated."

"Say, how'd you come out with Lori Crawford? Did she find any ghostly fingerprints?"

"She was tremendous. What she did was prove there are no ghosts. We've had more unexplainable activity in our upper room though. I was about to call you to tell you about it. It may even be a crime."

"Is it urgent, or can it wait until tomorrow?" Bloomfield asked. "I'm on my way out the door right now."

"It can wait, I'll call you tomorrow," I said as I heard Connie coming up the back stairs. I hung up the phone, kissed Connie's cheek and helped remove her jacket as she entered the room.

"I have a lot to tell you," I said.

"Oh, my. Good news or bad?"

"Two kinds of good."

"That sounds like news better heard on an empty bladder. Give me a second. I'll be right back." She returned and sat in the small rocker by the fireplace and said, "I'm ready. Talk."

"Sergeant Bloomfield was on the phone. They think they've caught the guy who mugged Lawrence."

"Well, praise the Lord! Who is he?"

"A guy who works at a fertilizer plant where they use anhydrous ammonia." I gave Connie all the details of my conversation with Bloomfield, paused, and asked, "Ready to turn the page?"

"Since its good news, I'm ready."

"You won't believe what happened during my meeting with Professor Woodside." It was my turn at theatrics as I pantomimed the pastor's performance. I didn't sit once. I made the imaginary vase fall, the perfumed air puff, and the photo tilt as dramatically as I could. Connie laughed.

"That's wonderful! But why?"

"I guess I must have seemed totally unnerved when Woodside found the Rebekah poem. He wanted to make sure I landed on the right side of the ghost question. I assured him we had.

Still, it was attention I didn't expect. Pastor Collins even volunteered to help us with a few ghost tricks of our own."

"Professor Woodside is a good one. You're lucky. But about the Rebekah limerick, what's our next move?" Connie asked.

"Clearly, someone is screwing with us," I said. "A living, breathing person who got up this morning, just like you and I, brushed his or her teeth, had a cup of coffee, scratched where it itches, and read the newspaper. Unlike us, the creep spent the rest of the day conjuring up new ways to harass people. Unfortunately, we are those people. We just don't know who or why or how they get in. For now, I think we should make a list of people who have access to our apartment. It could be a lot of people. All they need's a key."

"The Tuckers would top the list," Connie said.

"Yep. They know when we're not here, plus they have a key. And, at the risk of losing our deposit, I think we should install sliding-bolt locks on the doors, front and back. Next, I think we should figure out who can type. I'll bet Tuck can't and Margarite can. Plus, her hands might not be large enough to fill out a rubber glove, allowing a little bit of rubber to get caught in the space bar," I said.

"So, who else makes the list?" Connie asked.

"Who else do we know? Batty Matty, Ralph the pharmacist, Lawrence, and his mother, and maybe Sam. That's it. Of course, it could be someone we don't know at all, like a former tenant."

"Ralph can type. I watched him type my prescription label," Connie said. "He's fast too. Plus, he has access to rubber gloves."

"Still, I think the Tuckers seem like the place to start. I'm off to the hardware store to buy some locks."

"Wait a minute. I was here when I heard the typing. How'd the intruder get out of here without me noticing?"

"I don't know. Door bolts are just a start."

"Are we going to do this on our own?" Connie asked. "Why not let Bloomfield know what's going on?" Connie asked.

"You're right. I mentioned it to him. We've agreed to talk tomorrow."

I was beginning to enjoy the hunt.

Pariah Pastor

8

"WHY DON'T YOU LIKE butterscotch?" Connie asked.
"Geeze, I don't know. Why don't you like tuna fish?"
"Because it's cat food," Connie said as she laughed.

Connie and I enjoyed grocery shopping together. Our likes and dislikes were revealed long before we reached the dinner table, which was important on a fourth-grade teacher's salary. Even so, the trunk of my Chevy was full of groceries as we pulled into our back-alley parking spot alongside the Tucker's garage. We partially unloaded and walked across the backyard, arms full of grocery bags. Two more remained in the open trunk of the car. Margarite swung open her back door and waved at us with purpose.

"Oh, my goodness, you two have your hands full. Forgive me, but I'd like to talk with you if you have a moment," Margarite said.

"Sure. Let us put this stuff down first. This is only part of our load. Don't shop at King Soopers tonight. There's nothing left," I said. We placed the groceries at the foot of our stairs and cut across the lawn and stood before her porch. Margarite let the screen door slam behind her but remained on her top step.

"We've had a bright idea," she said, looking down at us. "After our conversation the other night, we started thinking. We'd like to put this ghost business behind us once and for all. We'd like to hire paranormal investigators to check the house."

"You want to do what?" Connie asked.

"You know, hire ghost hunters. They visit places reported to be haunted and run tests to determine if the haunting is real or nonsense. We're betting they'd come up totally empty here, and we could all rest easy. What do you think? We'd cover the costs."

"Well, I guess that'd be okay, probably pretty interesting, too." I said. "But I know nothing about it. What the heck to they do? I mean how long does it take? They have to stake the place out for hours, days, weeks, what?"

"Just hours, I think. I still have plenty to learn myself."

"Margarite, why don't you let us get our groceries in the house and think about this for a second," I said. "I'll call you right back. Is that okay?"

"That's fine. Just let me know. I'll set it up."

As we walked toward our steps and our groceries, Connie turned back to Margarite and asked, "Where do you find people like that?" She received no answer. Margarite had gone back inside. I helped Connie tote the groceries to our kitchen and returned to the car for the remaining two bags.

Connie had already placed the perishables in the fridge and sat at the kitchen table paging through the Yellow Pages when I returned.

"Need I ask what you are looking for?" I asked.

"Ghost hunters, of course."

"Find any?"

"Do you believe it. There are three of them listed under Paranormal Investigators."

"What's next and why now? If people have been complaining about spooks here for years, why do they just now decide to call the poltergeist police?"

"Better asked Margarite when you call her back."

"You know what? Before I call her, I'm going to call Pastor Collins."

"He's Professor Woodside's friend?"

"Yep, and he invited me to call him if I needed to."

I searched my wallet for his business card. *Pastor Archie Collins – Purveyor of GHOST STORIES – Spirited entertainment at its best.* Even though it was late in the day, I called. His wife answered and took a message.

I smiled at Connie and said, "Margarite will have to wait. I'm sure Pastor Collins will have some insight that will help."

He called back about seven-thirty that night.

"Hello Ron. Is your ghost misbehaving again?" he asked.

"No, our ghost has been very quiet recently. It's our landlady who has our attention. She wants to hire a professional to examine the house for paranormal activity."

"No kidding. How do you feel about that?"

"I'm unsure. Just seems weird."

"So do imagined ghosts. Who is she going to use, do you know?"

"I have no idea. Forgive me for being short on information," I said. "She mentioned it to us at a time when there was no time to get details. I need to call her back, and before I do, I wanted to talk to you. Do you know anything about these guys, these paranormal investigators? Are they the real deal?"

"Some are. Some aren't. Of course, there is no empirical evidence supporting the presence of ghosts. There's plenty of anecdotal stuff, but that is what it is. Still, some investigators have been at it a long time and are dedicated to the truth, but even they know it's impossible to study the question with scientific certainty. Most of the other guys, especially those who charge for their services, are well-practiced enthusiasts. What began as an interesting hobby became an obsession. So, as true believers, they need a way to support their addiction. I expect that's the level of help she'd be able to hire."

"So, there's no real reason to go ahead with this then, is there?" I looked at Connie with a reassuring smile.

Pastor Collins paused. "That depends, Ron. It depends on what questions you're trying to answer. You know there are no ghosts. But what you don't know is who is trying to make you believe otherwise. The process itself might overturn some stones you've walked past. Besides, it might be fun to watch. It's not every day you're invited to a real live ghost hunt. Forgive the oxymoron."

Connie noticed my quick smile and knew I had changed directions. "Well, there's a thought. And you're right. I have no need to confirm my skepticism about ghosts. But I can fake naive interest and do my own undercover research. That does sound like fun. How about joining me?"

"Ha! They'd never let me in. Denver's collection of paranormal dabblers is a small, loosely knit group. We all know one another or at least about one another, and my cynicism makes me a ghost-hunting pariah. It'd blow your cover wide open if I tagged along."

"Hmmm, Archie Collins, the pariah pastor, another oxymoron. Just one more question. What am I getting myself into? What will they do?"

"They all work a little differently but get ready to lose some sleep. Their sessions usually occur during the early-morning hours. They'll bring in some electronic equipment to measure and probe things like temperature and radiation levels. They'll have cameras and recorders, and usually one of the team members will have supernatural sensitivities. You know, a trance-medium type to serve as sort of a human divining rod."

"Wow. Sounds like quite a production, and one I probably shouldn't miss. Pastor, when I called, I was looking for a reason to say no. Now, I'm excited to give it a shot."

I called Margarite the next morning and allowed her to convince me that inviting strangers into her house to search for ghosts was a good idea.

"Well, okay then. Set it up," I said. "Connie and I are available almost any day after five. I guess both you and Tuck will join us?"

"I'm unsure how many spectators will be allowed, but you can be sure I'll be there," Margarite said. "Knowing Tuck, he'll probably decline. Let me see what I can do. I'll get back to you, and thanks for calling back, Ron."

Margarite called us back two days later. She had arranged for the ghost hunt, but we would have to wait for three weeks. Bump-in-the-Night Paranormal Investigators (BNPI) had no openings until then.

The First Corvette

9

ALMOST SEVEN WEEKS from the day of his mugging, Lawrence's cast was removed. Even with the windows shut on the crisp November morning, we heard him coming. "Bells and chimes are going to ring, Mamie Eisenhower, Mamie Eisenhower, Mamie Eisenhower." He wasn't headed for Glazier's. He was headed for our house. His mother asked us to keep an eye on Lawrence while she visited her ailing sister in Boulder on Saturday.

It was Lawrence's first time in the Cooperman House in almost twenty years. We could tell he was happy to return. His old buddy, Wally, wouldn't be here, but many memories would. He ascended the stairs to our living room with a slight limp and eyes wide beneath his orange Broncos cap.

"Lawrence. How about a donut?" Connie asked.

"Good, good, good!"

"Join me in the kitchen," Connie said.

We didn't skimp. Connie placed an oozing, jelly donut before him on our two-person kitchen table. Helping Hands cake donuts were not an option. Connie sat in one chair, Lawrence in the other. I stood by the kitchen counter nursing my cup of coffee. "How about something to drink, Lawrence? Coffee, milk, tea?"

"Milk, milk, milk."

I poured a glass of milk for him. "Lawrence, it's been a while since you've been here, I guess."

"Wally house, Wally house, Wally house." Lawrence said.

"Was Wally a good friend?" I asked.

"Good friend, good friend, good friend."

One jelly donut, a glass of milk, and four napkins later, we moved to the living room. "Well, Lawrence, your mom will be back to get you about noon. What shall we do this morning?" I asked. Lawrence up stood from his place on the couch, turned and pointed to the upper-room door. He walked to the door, turned, and pointed again toward the upper room.

"You want to go upstairs?" I asked. "Sure, we can do that. Let's go." I walked to the door and opened it, inviting him to lead the way. He took one look up the darkened stairway, found the light switch without searching, and turned on the light. He'd forgotten nothing. He climbed the stairs as I followed closely behind. Rather than turn and open the upper-room door, he walked straight to the landing wall and pushed hard against it with both palms. A narrow door we'd never seen bounced open, revealing a dark expanse of attic.

"Lawrence, what have you found?" I asked. "What have you found?"

He took one step inside the darkened space, pulled the string on the stud-mounted light, and illuminated a portion of the long, partially floored attic. Then he looked down and to the left and pointed toward the floor.

"Wally toys, Wally toys, Wally toys," he said.

I looked down at a lonely assortment of abandoned toys. A dump truck, miniature replica cars, a cap pistol, and a coffee can full of marbles rested amid the dust and the cobwebs.

"I take?" Lawrence asked.

"Sure, I guess," I answered, as I allowed my eyes to adjust and scan the attic darkness. A narrow strip of plywood flooring ran the length of the room. It was about four-feet wide, and where its edges stopped, joists and insulation began. An unidentifiable, low-slung, barred structure interrupted the fuzzy darkness at the end of the room. When I took a step toward it, Lawrence wouldn't have it.

"Danger, danger, danger," Lawrence said, warning me not to step further into the dimly lit space. Someone had taught him well. I would explore later. Lawrence picked up one of the replica cars, brushed it off, put it in his pocket and stepped back though the open door. I turned off the light and followed him.

He entered the upper room and went straight to the window and peered outside. Then he turned and examined my Underwood. I was dying to tell Connie what I'd found, but it seemed important to allow Lawrence to finish his tour. I spun a sheet of paper into the typewriter carriage and, still standing, typed his name several times. He read it and said, "Lawrence, Lawrence, Lawrence." I invited him to sit in front of the typewriter. He did and pounded out a line of random letters with his index fingers. The Underwood announced the line's end with its trustworthy ding. He tilted his head and faintly smiled. Careful not to touch him, I reached over his shoulder and returned the carriage. Lawrence pecked out another line. Ding. His subtle smile returned, and his upward glance asked permission to touch the carriage return handle. I nodded, and he gently pushed the carriage back to the starting position.

That seemed to satisfy him. He stood, stepped out of the small room, and began his limping descent to our living room. He said, "Connie Coop, Connie Coop, Connie Coop."

She heard him coming.

"Look what we found, Connie," I said. "Lawrence, show Connie Coop what you found."

He reached in his pocket and withdrew a miniature replica of a 1953 Corvette. He handed it to Connie and explained, "Wally toy, Wally toy, Wally toy."

Connie took it, glanced at it, and said, "Lawrence, that's wonderful." Her puzzled attention quickly bounced from the car to me.

"Lawrence showed me an attic room we didn't know we had. I'll show it to you later. But that's where we found some of Wally's missing toys. Lawrence, what would we do without you?"

He looked pleased, but extended his open hand to Connie, encouraging her to return his commemorative toy. She smiled and handed it back. To Lawrence it was a reminder of his friend Wally. To others, it was a trophy. It was an almost perfect replica of America's classic sportscar that took the automotive world by storm in 1953. Like the original, it was a convertible with no exterior door handles and was painted polo white with a contrasting red interior.

On that day, it remained a toy. Its tiny steering wheel turned the front wheels, and its hood opened. I built a little cardboard ramp for the Corvette to scoot over and crash. As much as he loved the recovered toy, three crashes later, Lawrence was ready to move on. I turned on the television, and he watched his favorite Saturday morning cartoons and a fishing program he liked. I knew it was a lazy way to entertain him, but it gave me a chance to spend a moment in the kitchen with Connie explaining more precisely what Lawrence had revealed.

We were both eager to explore the attic and were pleased when Lawrence's mother arrived just as the clock struck noon.

"Get the flashlight, Connie. You won't believe this," I said.

The secret door remained ajar. We both stepped carefully into the attic.

"Wow. Lawrence walked right to it, huh?" Connie asked.

"He bumped the door with both palms, and pow! the attic was revealed. Must have been a favorite place to play and hide stuff when Lawrence was hanging out with Wally. More recently, it may have served a different purpose. Let's see what we can see," I said as I aimed the flashlight toward the end of the room. Its help was minimal. The flashlight needed new batteries, and its anemic glow lit only the floor a few steps in front of us.

I led. We carefully walked almost the full length of the narrow walkway before the barred structure at the end of the room began to take shape. We saw a circular, wrought iron railing, protruding from the attic floor, the railing of a spiral staircase. It descended into utter darkness which instantly consumed our flashlight's feeble beam. We saw only two steps down and a bare lightbulb just below the attic floor opening. I looked for a switch but found none.

"Holy crap!" Connie said. "I think we've discovered Rebekah's Pass."

"Rebekah's Pass or that of one of our eccentric landlords." I peered over the railing and whispered loudly. "Margarite? Tuck? Are you down there?"

"You're not going down those stairs, are you?"

"Not with this puny flashlight. But I'm going down there."

"Ron, what's the matter with you? Let's call Bloomfield."

"I think the more people we get walking around up here the less likely we are to find the truth. I need more than new batteries. I need a headlamp."

"You need your head examined. That's what you need."

The Cooperman House mystery seemed to have switched our temperaments. We remained complementary, but she wanted to go slowly, and I wanted to charge ahead.

Walk Carefully

10

A N HOUR LATER, I returned to the attic with the lamp strapped comfortably to my forehead, my hands free to grasp the cold, winding railing of the spiral staircase. To my mind, a headlamp was one of the most practical emergency accessories you could buy. I wore tennis shoes to dampen the sound of my footsteps and a long-sleeved shirt to avoid the creepiness of cobwebs.

Connie stood at the top of the vertical tunnel armed with the handheld flashlight with brand new batteries. My headlamp did its duty as I wound my way down, but its success was very directional. Total darkness flanked me on three sides and amplified the silence and the claustrophobic stuffiness of the enclosure. I could hear the cushioned soles of my shoes meet the metal steps and the whispering friction of my right hand sliding down the handrail. I stopped often to listen for sounds other than mine. I heard none. The stairway itself was solid and surprisingly free of dust. I passed our floor at a spot I thought would be adjacent to our bedroom and bathroom.

We had noticed the thick wall between our bedroom and bathroom but paid no further attention. Now it made sense. The shaft for the spiral staircase was inside the wall and the brick protrusion on the outside of the house, which we thought was a capped chimney. I continued my descent past the Tucker's main floor and beyond. My shirt was damp with nervous perspiration as I reached the bottom and stepped into the closeted darkness. I found a light switch and turned it on. Naked forty-watt bulbs partially illuminated the twisting staircase. They were mounted on the wall near the railing at ten-foot intervals. As I looked up, an intermittent glow bounced off the spiraled steps and the brick walls of the shaft, but I couldn't see the top.

The enclosure where I stood had only one way forward. I turned and lowered my head to allow the lamp to shine on a spot where a door handle should be. There was no handle to turn, just a push pad to open the door from the inside and a small, metal handle to pull the door closed. I touched the push pad carefully, applying slow pressure as I held my breath. The door made a quiet click and open slowly, revealing a basement, a clean, slightly musty, everyday basement.

Ample light entered the room through a high window near the outside door. A wall, with a workbench and an ancient collection wall-mounted tools partially divided the room. Around the corner from the timeworn workbench, two gas furnaces and two water heaters stood guard before the boarded-up coal chute. A doorway, which I imagined led to the Tucker's main floor, interrupted the far wall, with a washer and dryer tucked next to it. It was an unremarkable basement and a perfect staging area for our "supernatural" visitor. I was tempted to snoop further but decided not to push my luck. However, before my assent to the attic, I checked the outside door, which led to a short flight of open-air steps and the backyard. The door wasn't locked.

I returned to the staircase closet, pulled the door shut, turned off the lights and climbed into the darkness, which was eerily penetrated by my bobbing headlamp. The steady, cautious climb up the staircase winded me, and I was delighted to see Connie's concerned face break into a smile as I reached the top.

"Well, how's Rebekah? Did she show you her geodes?" Connie asked.

"Oh, yes, and then some. She's a big flirt, but I could see right through her."

Connie rolled her eyes and flashed a quick, appreciative smile, then she sobered and asked, "Seriously, what did you find?"

I stepped from the staircase onto the attic's plywood floor and answered, "Three floors down, I found another concealed door and the basement." Then, speaking in a quivering, ghostly voice, I pressed my luck, "The very room where Rebekah Cooperman died from a smack to her head and a rock in her pocket."

"Stop with Rebekah Cooperman! What was there?"

"Just basement stuff. Tools and water heaters. I was going to poke around a little but decided against it. I did check the outside door. It wasn't locked. Coincidence? Don't know." I motioned toward the secret door on the other end of the attic, inviting Connie to walk ahead of me across the makeshift floor. Her questions continued as we walked.

"So, even outsiders who knew about the hidden staircase would have access?"

"Sure. If the door remains unlocked."

"Suppose the staircase was original equipment or added later?"

"Not sure. It was in good shape, though. No wobbly railings or treacherous steps."

As we stepped into the upper-room landing, Connie asked, "Now, are you ready to call Bloomfield?"

"I guess. He's probably the best person to ask about what to do next."

We didn't have to wait. Ten minutes later, Bloomfield called us with news of his own.

"Hello, Ron. Bloomfield here. We've made some progress on Lawrence's case. Is this a good time to talk?"

"Sure. But we were just about to call you. We've found the pathway of our paranormal visitor. I think you'll find it surprising. You need to see it. Could you come by?"

"I guess so. Later in the day, say five o'clock. My news can wait and might be better delivered in person anyway," Bloomfield said.

"Sounds good. We'll see you then."

To break up our wait for Bloomfield, I decided to walk to Glazier's for potato chips and toilet paper. "Cheaper at a grocery store," Connie said.

"I know. But I need a breath of fresh air."

I exchanged greetings with Matty, and, on a whim, I walked over to the prescription window to asked Ralph if he had any news about Connie's empty inhaler.

"Yes, I do. I've been meaning to call her." Using a small metal blade held in his practiced right hand, he continued to whisk pills into the grooved side of his counting tray and empty them into the prescription bottle as we talked. "I spoke with the manufacturer, and they admitted on rare occasions a bottle is released that is not adequately filled."

"Gosh, you'd think they'd have a process to check that. Well, thank you for checking. Next time it happens, we'll know what's up." As I checked out, Matty asked if we had news on Lawrence's mugger. I said no, with only a fleeting thought of telling Matty about our upcoming meeting with Bloomfield and his secret.

Ralph's dexterous hands were on my mind when I arrived at home. Connie was vacuuming in the living room when I walked in through the back door. She didn't hear me over the roaring old Hoover, so I entered the room with an exaggerated wave. She saw me and silenced the vacuum. "How is Batty Matty?" she asked.

"She's fine, and I talked with Ralph. He said the empty inhaler was the manufacturer's slipup," I said.

"Really. That's good to know, I guess. Is he going to find another manufacturer?"

"He didn't say. But, you know, I think you are right about his ability to type. His hands are so delicate and nimble. I watched him bottle pills while I was talking to him."

"I wonder how he is at climbing stairs?" Connie asked, as she secured the cord of the battered old vacuum and placed it in the closet. She walked into the kitchen and poured a cup of coffee. I joined her.

"That's a good question. Another good question, what does Tuck have against him? Maybe I'll ask Tuck. Won't do it in front of Margarite though. She'd jump square in front of that conversation for sure."

"You're chasing gossip, not facts, Mr. Forensic Psychologist."

"Gossip, ah gossip, that's where juicy motives like to hide," I responded.

"I suppose so. But let's focus on one thing at a time. We shouldn't take our eyes off the paranormal ball now that we have it bouncing down a spiral staircase."

"I'm as interested in Bloomfield's response to the staircase as I am in his news," I said.

The doorbell rang. Bloomfield was twenty minutes early. "Hello, folks. Sounds like we've both been working overtime," he said, as he entered the living room.

"Please sit down, Sergeant. Can I get you something to drink?" Connie asked.

"I'm good. Thanks." He took a place on the couch. I sat in the small rocker by the fireplace. Connie chose the occasional chair near the couch.

"We have something to show you, and you have something to tell us. You go first. Ours might take a moment," I said.

"Okay, but hang on to your hats," Bloomfield smiled. "The name of the man who attacked Lawrence is Reginald Tucker. He's your landlords' son."

"What? Tuck and Margarite's son? Tuck mentioned he had a son, but it sounded like they were estranged. How did you find out who he was?" I asked.

"He told us. He told us everything. His childhood home wasn't happy. He and his dad went toe-to-toe over every decision Reggie made for years. I felt there was more to it, but he hasn't seen or spoken to his parents for over five years. He was feeling guilty I guess, plus, he needed money. Which came first, the guilt or the empty wallet, I don't know. Anyway, he'd been circling his old neighborhood in that beat-up Jeep trying to find courage enough to knock on their front door. That's when he saw Lawrence trudging along in the snow. It was a crime of opportunity. He attacked Lawrence for his money."

"What made him think Lawrence had money?" Connie asked.

"I'm getting to that," Bloomfield said and slowed Connie's questioning with a raised index finger. "He knew Lawrence from his growing-up years. He was ambivalent about him and always had been. To him, Lawrence was just the village idiot who was always there but never of interest. To Reggie, Lawrence could have been a fireplug."

"Sounds like a charming young man," Connie said

Bloomfield raised his eyebrows and nodded. "Reggie remembered one thing about Lawrence; he always had money in his wallet," Bloomfield said directly to Connie. "He knew because his dad knew. Lawrence used to sit on the front steps and talk with Mr. Tucker. Sometimes, Lawrence took out his wallet to show him pictures of his dad, his ID card, and other special things. Mr. Tucker took note of the cash and complained about how foolish it was for Mrs. Stroud to allow Lawrence to carry cash.

"Reggie parked his Jeep, grabbed a tire iron and attacked. With a little cash, he could postpone his meeting with his parents."

"He admitted all this? Sounds open and shut, doesn't it?" I asked.

"Yeah, but you never know. A good lawyer can do wonders."

"Do his parents know yet?" Connie asked.

"Yes. His mom visited him. His dad chose not to come."

"Wow, looks like Tuck had better warm up his geodes," I said.

"What?"

"Oh, just another little mystical experience we've had at Cooperman House. We visited with the Tuckers not long ago to talk about our ghostly concerns. While we were there, we noticed his collection of geodes on the shelves beside his fireplace. He didn't exactly say he trusted their guidance, but he was aware of what he called their metaphysical properties."

Connie stood, walked toward the front window, turned and said, "This has to be such a shock to the Tuckers. I don't trust either one of them, but I can't help feeling sorry for them. What should we do?"

"Of course, I don't know how well you know them, but I expect a response from anyone but close friends could be touchy, at least right now," Bloomfield said.

"I couldn't agree more," I said. "Especially after what we stumbled onto this morning. Is it my turn?"

"Whatcha got?"

I told him about my meeting with Professor Woodside, showed him the poem, and pointed out the void on the capital M. "It was typed on my typewriter," I said. Then I explained our morning with Lawrence and the spiral staircase. "Let me show you." I stood, put on my headlamp, and walked to the upstairs door. Bloomfield and Connie followed without saying a word. The hidden door bounced opened with one firm push, and we stepped inside the attic.

"Walk carefully," I advised. "The flooring strip is narrow."

Bloomfield placed his hands on the spiral staircase railing and peered into the unsettling, darkness. "Did you go down?"

"Yes, I did. It goes all the way to the basement. The light switch is at the bottom, so going down without first coming up requires a serious flashlight. That's why I bought this," I said, pointing proudly at my headlamp.

"Interesting. Let me see your lamp."

"You going down?" Connie asked.

"No, not all the way. I'd need a warrant for that. I'd just like a closer look at the stairs." Bloomfield held the lamp in his hand and walked down the first four steps of the staircase. He squatted and shined the light on the railing and on the steps above him and below him. He paid particular attention to the edges of the steps.

He looked up at us from his cramped staircase squat. "Thing's sturdy enough. Whoever built it knew what they were doing. You've only been down and back up one time, right?"

"Right," I said.

"There's been more traffic on these stairs than just you. The edges of the steps are dusty. The centers are not. It isn't a ghost. What sort of ghost uses steps anyway?" Bloomfield asked as he looked up and smiled. He returned to the attic floor. "What's down there?"

"Just a basement, a normal basement behind a hidden door. I didn't stay long. I did check the outside door. It wasn't locked. If it's always unlocked, our list of possible intruders lengthens."

"Yes, indeed."

"So, we have two questions. First, is our ghost breaking the law? Second, what should we do next?" I asked.

"Yes, the ghost is breaking the law. Which law will depend on who it is. If it's either of the Tuckers, they have the right to check for bats in their attic. They don't have the right to enter your rented space without cause. Nor do they have the right to harass you. If it's someone from the outside, they are breaking and entering, plain and simple. What's next? That's up to you. What's your goal? Do you just want to stop the ghostly visits, or do you want someone to be punished for harassing you?"

"Good question. I guess I want to know who's doing it. And I want them to stop. Punishment isn't important to me," I said. "What do you think, Connie?"

"I agree. Plus, I'd also like to know why. I mean, what sort of perverse thrill does someone get out of scaring people?"

"Well, we can probably find out who's doing it. We may never know why," Sergeant Bloomfield said.

"What if we just wanted it to stop?" I asked.

"What are you suggesting?" Bloomfield asked.

"Let's seal the staircase. We've blocked entry to our living space with sliding bolts on our doors. Why not do something similar with the staircase? Can you imagine someone tiptoeing across the basement floor and opening the secret door to their spiral staircase, only to be greeted by an eight-foot sheet of quarter-inch plywood? Touché, Rebekah!"

"So, you want to make a game of it rather than stop it? It's beyond game time for me," Connie said as she began her careful walk back across the attic floor. The detective followed and I followed him. No one spoke again until we were seated in the living room.

"I think Connie's right," Bloomfield said. "Messing with your 'ghost' sounds like fun, but it could come back to bite you. You'd be violating their space. Even if you sealed the door on your end, you'd be drilling holes in someone else's property. Of course, that assumes it's the Tuckers who are the spooks. If it's someone from the outside, the Tuckers might be happy to know about it."

"We can't know that until we catch them," Connie said.

"Or have evidence that points us in the right direction. Let me run this up the flagpole at headquarters. They'll be able to give me a certain assessment of laws broken. That might help us decide about next steps."

"Here's a thought," I said. "You still have Reggie Tucker in custody, right? Why not have another talk with him. Drop a couple of staircase hints and see where he takes you. If he knows about it, it's safe to believe his parents do too."

"I could make that happen."

"Also, Connie wondered when the staircase was built. If it is original equipment, the Tuckers might not know about it. Highly unlikely, but it is very well disguised, so it's possible. If it is newer, maybe installed when the Tuckers converted the house into two units, they must know. Are there architectural records available? You know, building permits and blueprints, that kind of thing."

"You'd be lucky to find anything beyond twenty years old. I've been down that road," Bloomfield said. Another option is to have an expert examine the stairs. A construction pro might give us an approximate date of manufacture and installation."

"Know anybody like that?" I asked.

"Yeah, but I don't want to call him until we know more."

"That makes sense."

"Could take me a couple of days to work through the things on my end. Must make sure I talk to the right people. Can you be patient that long?"

"Rebekah Cooperman hasn't rested easy since 1941. If she can wait, so can we," I said. Connie agreed.

"One more thing, Sergeant," I said. "And I hesitate to tell you this for fear you'll think we are nuts for considering it. Margarite wants to hire a team of paranormal investigators to search the house for supernatural residents. We told her to set it up, mostly for the fun of it. Of course, that was before we knew about Rebekah's secret passage. What do you think?"

"Paranormal investigators come in two flavors: charlatan delight or delusional swirl. Who's paying for it?"

"She is."

"Sure, go ahead. But expect nothing more than lost sleep. And you probably should wear your duck boots. You'll need them."

Hook, Line, and Poltergeist

11

I DECIDED TO BE FIRST to tell Matty of the identity of Lawrence's mugger, and I wanted to do it in person. Chances were, she knew Reggie Tucker. When I entered Glazier's, Matty was with a customer. I hung back, picked up a newspaper, and waited. When she was free, I placed the paper on the counter.

"Hi Matty. I've got some news for you. Got time to talk a moment?" I asked.

"Sure, Ron. What's up?"

"They've caught Lawrence's mugger. You may know him. His name is Reginald Tucker."

She furrowed her brow and peered over the top of her half-lensed glasses as she exclaimed, "What!"

"Reggie Tucker, Tuck and Margarite's son, is the guilty party," I repeated.

"I'll be. I haven't seen the guy for years. Haven't missed him much. He was a strange one. Distant, you know. But why would he mug Lawrence?"

"Sergeant Bloomfield told us it seemed like a crime of opportunity. He'd come back to reunite with his family and ask for some money. He saw Lawrence and decided Lawrence's money was an easier way to go," I explained, and then asked, "So, you knew him? Guess his folks hadn't seen him for years. What was going on there? Do you know?"

"Who knows? Margarite? She's an enigma. She plays the fool at times, but I don't think she is. Not by a long shot. And Tuck, well, he's always enjoyed being opinionated and disagreeable. He'll take you up his bitchy path as far as he can before he lets you rest. It's just plain fun for him." Matty hesitated, removed her glasses, and let them rest next to her name tag. "If Reggie had issues with someone, I'd guess it was his dad. It's not hard for me to imagine what kind of a hard, unforgiving parent he might have been. But Reggie, he was a smart kid but sort of off-center. Like I said, distant. I couldn't tell if he was angry or just sad. But, damn, I never figured him for something like this."

"Fortunately, Lawrence seems to be doing fine. I just thought you'd want to know about this development. If I learn more, I'll let you know." I paid for the newspaper and took a step toward the door.

"Thank you, Ron. I appreciate it. Goodness, you've had a rugged initiation into the neighborhood, haven't you?"

I turned toward Matty and smiled as I answered, "Interesting may be a better word. And you don't know the half of it." I kicked myself as soon as I said it. I still thought of Matty as a friend, and she was the last on my list of suspects but talking with her about our haunting was not something I could do.

Matty didn't hesitate. "Not the half of it? What else is going on?" she asked.

"Oh, you know. New schools, new jobs always come with surprises," I lied.

"I'm sure they do. I'm just glad your empty inhaler turned out to be nothing more mysterious."

I'd opened the supernatural door and needed to close it. "Oh, you mean like ghosts? Connie told me what you said about the Cooperman place. Gosh, Matty, if there's a spook over there, he must be scared to death of us. He's been as quiet as a mouse."

"Well, good. Hope she stays that way. Thanks for the update on Lawrence."

"You're welcome. There will be more, I'm sure. I'll keep you posted."

Matty's gender-changed reference to our visitor was not surprising. Of course, she knew about Rebekah Cooperman. Why wouldn't she call the ghost "she" after I called it "he"? It was her eagerness to swing the conversation toward the supernatural I found interesting. She was either a believer in paranormal phenomena who wanted to keep an eye on us out of genuine concern or she had a curiosity itch because of her involvement in a scheme to frighten us.

I was right about one thing. There was more to come. Margarite was allowed to pay Reggie's five-thousand-dollar bail on one court-approved condition, which even cantankerous Tuck had to agree to. Reggie was to be under house arrest in his parents' home. Reggie didn't want to go.

His resistance to the court-ordered homestay gave Bloomfield a perfect opportunity for his second interview and nonchalant staircase inquiry. Two days after we'd shown him the spiral staircase, Bloomfield called to update us on his second conversation with Reggie Tucker.

"I snuck the staircase mention into a normal conversation, and it worked," Sergeant Bloomfield said. "I asked Reggie if he was sure he didn't want to move home. He said he was certain. Then I suggested it seemed a better place to live than a jail cell or his rundown trailer and mentioned some of the advantages of the grand old house, like the great neighborhood, the extra space, home-cooked food, and the neat old spiral staircase."

"And he took the bait?" I asked.

"Yes sir, hook, line, and poltergeist. He sat back in his chair and looked at me as if I had revealed his most tightly held secret. He hesitated, leaned forward with his palms on the table between us, and asked, 'You know about the staircase?'

"He claimed only he and his mother knew about the staircase. When he asked me how I'd found out about it, I sort of blew it off. I told him the staircase wasn't as big a secret as he thought, and I asked if he was certain his dad didn't know. He said it was possible, but he had never talked with his dad about it, only his mom, and she always told him not to talk about it with anybody. I asked if he'd ever climbed the stairs. He said his mom wouldn't allow it. I didn't force the issue. I just suggested again his home was a better place to hang his hat than a jail cell. Then he reminded me that a jail cell's biggest, single advantage was the absence of his parents. No question, whatever trouble he had with his folks is still smoldering."

"So, we know Margarite knew about it. Tuck probably knew about it. Reggie knew about it as a boy. And we know Reggie's loathing continues," I said. "I wonder if Reggie can type."

"Now, despite what he wants, he'll probably have to move home. How do you feel about him living one floor beneath you?" Bloomfield asked.

"We're disappointed," I said. "We're concerned about Lawrence. What were they thinking, placing Reggie in a location just a few houses from his victim? What's going to keep him there?"

"Phone calls every day. And any time of the day. And he'd better be there or he's off to the big house . . . not just the county jail, but state prison."

Connie and I didn't like it at all, and I let Bloomfield know. "It sounds like his relationship with his folks could be explosive.

We hope there's no fallout that drifts our way. Think the court will respect his decision not to move home?"

"I doubt it."

He was right. Reggie became our new neighbor.

A Trigger Object

12

WE THOUGHT ABOUT CANCELLING our participation in the ghost hunt, but there were still too many questions. Plus, the timing was perfect. We would attempt to contact the troubled spirit of Rebekah Cooperman just a week after we discovered a secret passage that led to the place of her death. We could only speculate on Margarite's motives. She either honestly wanted to prove there was no ghost in her house or she wanted to add to our supernatural angst. But, if so, why? And who else knew about the spiral staircase? We decided to play dumb and go through with Margarite's plan, a plan she was cheerfully executing. She invited us to meet with a representative of BNPI two days before the event.

The meeting began in the Tuckers' living room. BNPI owner, Arlo Schneider, explained the ghost hunt agenda to Margarite, Connie, and me. Tuck wasn't there, and Reggie remained in his room.

We sat in chairs, but Arlo sat on a three-legged stool in front of the fireplace. "I'm here to explain what will occur next Tuesday morning and to answer your questions. Margarite convinced us this house is worthy of exploration, and we'll do our best to make contact with resident spirits, if they are here."

He was a clean-shaven, slender man of about thirty, wearing unscuffed hiking boots, professionally pressed jeans, and a navy-blue turtleneck with a small BNPI logo. He spoke easily and with conviction, perched on his stool in front of the fireplace and Salvador Dali's headless Jesus.

"There'll be four of us. I'll handle the photography. My technical assistant, Jimmy, will operate the audio recorder and the ambient temperature gun. Colder spots can indicate the presence of spirit beings. Ghosts require energy to be seen or heard, and they take that energy from the air, causing a localized drop in air temperature. And Lavera. Lavera's a clairvoyant. As a medium, she has special sensitivities that help us confirm the presence of unseen souls. And last, but not least, is Dexter. Dexter's a cat with his own built-in sensitivities. I hope nobody is allergic to cats?"

No one raised their hand. Cats could cause Connie's asthma to flair up, but it only occurred after an extended exposure. We didn't mention it, which allowed Arlo to continue without breaking stride.

"Good. Like I said, Dexter has his own sensitivities. If he sits and stares at a particular area, it helps us know where to concentrate our search."

Arlo smiled and stepped from his stool. "It all sounds spooky weird, doesn't it? It really isn't. It's just a peek into another dimension that exists whether we believe it or not. The thing is, it's only seen if you look very hard. That's all we're doing. We've been working together for over six years. Sometimes we connect with spirits in undeniable ways. Sometimes we draw blanks. But ghosts are as real as this fireplace," Arlo said as he stepped to the fireplace and rapped his knuckles on the mantel. "Any questions so far?"

Cooperman House

"Do we all get to watch you work?" I asked.

"Yes. My usual spectator limit's two, but Margarite said it's important for you and Connie to join her. Both of you are more than welcome. Actually, during the hunt, you all become part of the team."

"So, Tuck isn't coming?" I asked Margarite.

"No, he'll be out of town."

"That's a shame. If we connect with a ghost, he'll never believe it."

"I know," Margarite said. "Strong opinions often come with blinders. It's you two I'm worried about. Not Tuck." Her head twitched for the first time that night.

"Mr. Schneider, how long does this take?" Connie asked.

Arlo smiled and said, "Please, call me Arlo. Formalities promote distance. Remember, you're a team member. It's important that we're as likeminded as possible, you know, open, eager, and unresistant. To answer your question, it'll probably take about two hours. We'll start at two a.m. and search until about four a.m. It could vary depending upon how things go."

"Will you work in only our apartment or the entire house?" I asked.

"We'll start in your apartment but spend most of our time in the basement where Rebekah Cooperman was killed. That's where we'll place the trigger object."

"Trigger object? What's that?" Connie asked.

"It's any object that may have special meaning to our subject. In this case, we'll use one of these," Arlo said. He reached for an unbroken geode on the bookshelf behind him. "This'll work perfectly," he said. He held the rough, golf-ball sized stone in his palm and passed it before us. Then he placed it on the stool's seat. "We'll place this stool and the geode front and center and hope it encourages contact."

"The rock in her pocket, right?" I asked.

96

"Right. We're guessing it's a lot like Rebekah's."

"What else?" Arlo asked. We were all quiet, so he continued. "A couple more things. Please wear dark clothing and soft-soled shoes. If there's a visual response from Rebekah, it'll probably be quick. We don't want to be distracted by our own presence. Likewise, if it's an audible signal, like tapping or even a voice, we want to hear it and not the shuffle of our own footsteps. Okay, we'll see you early Tuesday morning. If you have other questions, please call me." Arlo handed each of us a business card.

"Margarite, is there anything we can do to help you set up?" I asked.

"Thanks, Ron. You know, we'll need that stool and folding chairs in the basement. If you could help me with that it would be great."

"Add a chair for Lavera, please," Arlo said. "She works best when she's sitting."

I called Pastor Collins the next morning.

"Pastor, I have a couple questions for you. Do you have a moment?"

"Sure. Got a date set for your ghost hunt?"

"Yep. Next Tuesday morning, early. We met with the ghost-hunter team yesterday for a briefing. Something came up I thought was unusual. They're bringing a cat. What about that?"

"Not unusual. Cats are used sometimes. Dogs even. Most often cats. Supposedly, spirit-sensitive cats just sit and stare in the direction of detected ghosts. Of course, the cat could just as easily be showing interest in an open can of tuna fish behind the wall."

"Okay, so nothing unusual. What about trigger objects? Ever heard of those?"

"Sure. Going to wake up Rebekah with the hammer that hit her?"

"No, a geode, like the one she had in her pocket when she died," I said, then took a breath before asking Pastor Collins a for favor I knew was out-of-bounds. "Just one more question. First, let me set it up. Imagine an unbroken geode sitting on a three-legged stool in the middle of the basement where Rebekah was killed. There sits the trigger object, with team members busily doing their thing to make contact with Rebekah when, suddenly, the geode falls off the stool and rolls across the floor, sort of like the red vase that fell off the shelf in Professor Woodside's office. Wouldn't their reaction be priceless?"

"So, you want to know how to make a geode fall off a stool?"

"Yes, I know I'm asking you to reveal a trade secret, but wouldn't it be a great way to test the integrity of the ghost hunters and the motives of our landlady?"

"Couple ways to do it. Monofilament line is the simplest. Go to a fly-fishing shop and buy Maxima Chameleon monofilament line. Four pound should work. It's hair thin, surprisingly strong, and changes color to match its environment. Affix it to the leg of the stool. String the line across the floor to where you'll be standing or sitting. When you are properly positioned, bend down to tie your shoe, and entangle the line in the knot. When the time is right, change the position of your foot in a gentle and inconspicuous way and watch the geode tumble."

"Takes some planning, doesn't it?"

"Yes, it does. And it works best in a controlled environment. It'll be tougher if you're not sure where you'll be stationed in the room. You see, it's all very practical, unmagical stuff. At times, gravity is a magician's best friend. Just remember, magic only occurs when things remain unseen. Find a way to gather and secure the line when all is said and done."

"Thank you, Pastor Collins. Thank you. I have some work to do. I'll keep you posted."

I helped Margarite set up the basement room that afternoon. We moved the chairs and the stool downstairs. The workbench half of the room was larger and away from the furnaces, so we placed the chairs there. They formed a semicircle in front of the stool holding Rebekah's trigger object, which stood a few feet in front of the secret-door wall.

Late that night I snuck into the basement through the unlocked backyard door to tie the undetectable monofilament line to the leg of the stool. I moved the geode to the workbench, so it didn't fall while I worked, and I aimed my headlamp down the stool's leg nearest the wall. I knelt, looped the line around the leg three times, and slid it down close to the floor before finishing the knot. To my surprise and temporary disappointment, someone had beaten me to it and tied their own monofilament rip cord to the leg of the stool. It wasn't Maxima Chameleon, but there it was. The trailing end of the line led directly to the chair nearest the outer wall, the chair that was supposed to be mine.

I had reveled in the thought of shocking Margarite and the ghost hunters with Rebekah's falling geode, but I was quick to understand the advantages of being late to the stool. I wouldn't have to worry about jockeying into position to lay claim to the surreptitious chair and, more important, whoever took the seat would be revealed as a ghost-hunting counterfeit.

The stool was sculpted for comfortable sitting, with slight contours to match the posterior of the sitter. I returned the geode to its precarious perch, making sure that it rested on the sloping side of the seat.

The next night, just a little before two a.m., we watched headlight beams roll to a slow stop in front of the house and go out. Moments later, Margarite called to tell us the BNPI team had arrived and asked if we could begin the search in our apartment. To avoid waking Reggie, the team stood in our living room. Arlo, Jimmy, Lavera and caged Dexter were ready to begin their search. Margarite, Connie, and I were ready to watch. Arlo wore black tennis shoes rather than hiking books.

After a round of introductions, Arlo said, "Well, folks, welcome to the team. Whatever happens, we think it will be a night worth losing sleep over. Just a final thought before we begin. Please be silent. There'll be time to talk after we're done, so please refrain from sharing your thoughts until we've finished. You'll hear the three of us talking when we must. It won't happen often. But it is necessary. And, if we do have questions of you, please keep your answers short."

"Okay, everyone ready? If you've had your coffee and used the bathroom, let's get started." Arlo released Dexter. The large, long-haired, cat stepped out of his cage as if he owned the apartment. He was solid black, except for his white front feet.

"We'll just let Dexter roam. He's a twenty-pound Maine Coon, and he's as smart as he is large. If we see him showing special interest in anything we'll show special interest too."

Jimmy knelt beside his equipment bag and retrieved his portable tape recorder and his pistol-gripped thermometer, which he plugged into the battery pack strapped to his hip. He was younger than the other two. Probably in his early twenties, with shaggy, blond hair crushed beneath a sweat-stained ball cap with a BNPI logo. He nodded at Arlo and Lavera, indicating his readiness.

Lavera hadn't said a word. Even when we met her, she only smiled. A prematurely grey woman in her early thirties, she had noticeably smooth, ivory skin and striking blue eyes. She carried herself with quiet confidence and was perfectly suited for her shin-length, contour-hugging black dress, which was loosely sashed at the waist. She returned Jimmy's nod.

"Okay team, here we go. Ron, please turn out the lights," Arlo said. I flipped the switch by the kitchen door and the room went almost dark, illuminated only by a lonely streetlight and the moon. Arlo turned on his headlamp, and I immediately wished I had mine. He examined the living room from wall to wall, turned off his headlamp, and said, "Okay, Jimmy. Record and measure. Lavera, concentrate." Minutes passed as Jimmy walked the room with the green glow of his handheld thermometer reflecting upward across his face. Lavera was silent. Jimmy completed his trip around the room, turned off his meter, and said, "Nothing."

Arlo took the lens cap off his Nikon and snapped images of each wall and one of each corner. The flash of his last shot revealed the team member I'd forgotten. Dexter sat quietly in front of the door to the upper room. His resolute stare at the door was unaltered when Arlo spoke.

"Where's that door lead?" Arlo asked.

"Upstairs to my study room," I answered.

"Dexter wants us to go up there. May I lead the way?"

"Sure, light switch is on the right-hand wall. Turn left at the top of the stairs."

"Just flashlights for now. Jimmy has another. He'll bring up the rear."

Even though enough moonlight shone through the blindless window to allow us to see well enough not to step on one another, six people and a twenty-pound cat stuffed into the upper room was uncomfortable. Arlo asked us to give his associates room to work. Connie and Margarite stepped out of the room. I stood in the doorway. Jimmy repeated the temperature measurement, and Lavera sat at my desk with her hands on my typewriter. She was clicking but she wasn't typing. It sounded as though she was snapping her tongue on the roof of her mouth at half-second intervals. She stopped and started again, this time the tongue snaps were replaced by a faster guttural clucking sound that echoed down her throat. I turned my head toward Arlo. Even in the dim light, he noticed and raised his hand, indicating the need for patience. Finally, she stopped, dropped her head and shoulders in a moment of clairvoyant fatigue. Arlo snapped pictures and turned on his headlamp. Dexter sat on the windowsill staring at the moon.

"Lavera, are you back?" Arlo asked.

"Yes," she said.

"Anything?"

"Death speaks in whispers," she said.

"Well, that's something. Good," Arlo said. "Ron you can turn on the lights. Let's go to the basement."

I turned on the lights, still afraid Dexter was going to stake out a spot directly in front of the secret attic door. Luckily, he was first to leave the upper room and run down the stairs. We all followed his fluffy tail to our living room. Jimmy gently placed him in his cage, and we made our way to the basement down our backyard stairs.

Margarite and I led the single-file march down the stairs to the basement. Still curious about Tuck's absence, I whispered, "Where is Tuck, anyway?"

"Golf outing in Phoenix. We just couldn't make our schedules dovetail this time. He'll be home late tomorrow."

"Shame," I said again as we entered the basement.

The folding chairs, the stool, and the geode were just as I'd left them. This was the moment of truth. Arlo's earlier request for Lavera's chair could have had a veiled purpose. Perhaps he needed someone to pull the trigger object's trigger. Margarite, the organizer, was always a suspect. Whoever sat in the chair nearest the wall was our charlatan. Connie and I waited to sit until Lavera and Margarite chose their seats. Lavera chose a chair directly in front of the stool. Margarite skirted the room and casually eased into the condemning chair. Connie sat to the right of Lavera. I decided to stand.

"Okay, gang. Here we go. Jimmy, release Dexter and let's begin," Arlo said as he turned out the lights with the wall switch nearest the door and made his way back to the front of the room. He turned off his headlamp. A meager dusting of diffused moonlight sifted through the narrow basement window. Our eyes adjusted to the basement darkness slowly, and the reflected green light across Jimmy's face seemed much brighter than it had upstairs. Lavera began clicking and clucking immediately. Jimmy explored the entire basement and finished with two cold spots detected. He didn't speak but held up two fingers alongside the glow of his temperature gun and pointed to the hidden-door wall. Then he stepped toward the furnace side of the room and pointed toward the boarded-up coal chute. Arlo readied his camera but didn't take pictures. Dexter jumped up on Connie's lap and purred.

"Alright, let's just sit quietly for a while to see if we can connect," Arlo said. Lavera's meditative noises continued for thirty anxious seconds and stopped. Dexter's gentle, rolling purr was the only sound until Lavera spoke. Her hollow, monotone voice chilled the room. "Someone is here," she said.

We all heard it. A door slammed. Footsteps ensued, then stopped and started again.

Silence returned. A voice came from upstairs, "Reggie, where's your mom?" There was a muffled answer.

"Margarite! Where the hell are you? Tuck tromped across the kitchen floor, opened the basement door, and yelled, "Margarite, you down there?"

"Oh, for Christ's sake," Margarite hissed. "What's he doing home?" She rose and rushed to the foot of the stairs, and yelled, "Yes, Tuck. I'm down here. And don't you dare come down here. I'm in the middle of something."

Tuck charged down the stairs, turned on the light and stared at the assemblage before him. "What the hell is going on here?" he shouted. "Who are these people!"

It was Margarite's place to answer, but she didn't. Arlo did, "Hello, I'm Arlo Schneider and this is my team. We're paranormal investigators, here to search for the spirit of Rebekah Cooperman." He walked across the room and handed Tuck his business card.

Tuck glanced at the card, walked toward the workbench section of the room, and stopped. He saw people he knew and people he didn't, all dressed in dark clothing, paying homage to a rock on a stool, plus, there was a twenty-pound cat sitting on Connie's lap. He hesitated, then sneered his way into a thundering tirade.

"Well, I'll be damned, a supernatural shyster right here in my basement, an honest-to-god ghost detective stands before me in the flesh." Tuck glanced at Arlo's card again and said, "Well, Mr. Arlo Ghost-Dick Schneider, let me tell you who I am. I'm the pissed off ghost of a rectal surgeon and I'm an expert at making assholes disappear. I want you to get your phony ass out of my house right now!"

Arlo didn't hesitate. "We are leaving. Mr. Tucker, I am so sorry we took you by surprise. Okay gang, gather your stuff. It's time to go. Margarite, mail me your check." It took a moment to find and cage Dexter, who'd jumped off Connie's lap and hidden beneath the workbench during Tuck's outburst. With that done, the BNPI team escaped out the backyard basement door.

"Ron, Connie, you two in on this?" Tuck asked.

"Tuck, we were invited to attend. That's all. Margarite invited us, claiming she wanted to answer the ghost question once and for all. Naturally, we came, and we're going home now and let you two sort things out," I said. Connie and I followed Arlo out the basement door.

Ferocious Tiger

13

A FULL DAY PASSED. We minded our own business, thinking it wise to let the Tuckers cool a little before we forced the issue. We were ready with a complete list of damning questions and accusations and were confidently patient. If they didn't invite a conversation the next day, we would take the initiative. As it turned out, a raucous discussion about the staircase and the dubious ghost hunt was forced upon all of us later that night.

We were awakened by loud, metallic clanging at four o'clock in the morning. Regularly spaced, reverberating clanks of metal against metal rose from beneath us. Starting and stopping, echoing upward, loudly, and deliberately. "What is that?" Connie asked, unsure if she was awake or dreaming. "Do you hear it?"

"Of course, I hear it. The whole damned house must hear it. Sounds like it must be coming from the basement or the staircase."

"Holy crap! What next? What do we do?"

"Let's give it a second."

Two more rounds of three-strike clanks drifted upward. Then they slowed. They became weaker and less evenly spaced. Still audible. Still troubling.

"Someone's trying to spook us again or someone's in trouble!" I said. "Either way, I've got to go down there."

"Down the attic stairs? That's just crazy."

"Not those stairs. I'm going down the back stairs and through the backyard entrance. Hope it's unlocked." I jumped out of bed, forced my legs into my jeans and quickly tied my sneakers. "If it isn't open, I'm going to make so much noise Tuck and Margarite will think someone stepped on a land mine in their backyard."

I snatched my headlamp from the dresser and ran through the kitchen and bounded down the outdoor stairs and the steps to the basement. The door was unlocked. I entered and reached for the light switch. Before I found it, the lights came on and Tuck appeared. He'd come down the kitchen stairs wearing slippers and a magnificently decorated black silk kimono over his pajamas. A ferocious, embroidered tiger came toward me through a delicate scattering of sky-blue flowers and wispy green foliage. It was armed with a fireplace poker.

"Tuck. What the hell is that noise?" I asked, with no concern about barging uninvited into his basement.

"I have no idea," he said.

"Let's find out," I said. I walked directly to the north wall and pushed the secret door with both hands. It popped open and slowly swung on its hidden hinge to reveal the staircase closet.

As the door opened Tuck gasped, "Holy shit! What the hell is this?"

"It's a hidden staircase. Surely you knew about it."

"I had no idea," Tuck said. "This is just crazy and how the hell did you know about it?"

"Rebekah told me, Tuck."

The sting of my sarcasm vanished as we peered inside and saw the source of the clanking. Blood pooled around a rubber-gloved hand, which lay on the floor alongside a dented metal flashlight. A limp arm dangled from a slow-breathing torso, which stretched upside down across the twisting, lower steps of the spiral staircase. As I shined the headlamp toward the ascending stairs, I saw a khaki-clad leg stretched taut and entangled in the steps. The right ankle was twisted between the edge of a step and a vertical handrail support. The injured man seemed vaguely aware of our presence and raised his blood-matted head and turned it slightly. It was Ralph.

Tuck exploded, "What the hell, Ralph! You philandering little pervert, what are you doing in my basement?"

"We'll figure that out later, Tuck. Right now, we've got to get him out of there. He's bleeding like a stuck pig," I said as I squeezed past Ralph, climbed up four steps, and examined his mangled ankle. "Can you lift him a little to relieve the pressure on his leg?"

Still seething, Tuck dropped the poker, pulled up his silk sleeves, and stepped around the pooled blood. He grabbed Ralph's shoulders and lifted. His effort gave no relief. The two inches of lift Tuck gave him was consumed by Ralph's already overextended joints. He was a weighted Slinky toy, unable to recoil.

"Tuck, I need an adjustable crescent wrench. Got one?"

"I think so." He shuffled to the workbench, grabbed a rusty wrench from its pegboard perch, and handed it to me. "This okay?"

"That'll do. I'm going to loosen the step if I can. Go back upstairs and call an ambulance. Then come back. We've got some work to do. And bring a couple of towels. We've got to stop the bleeding."

The nuts on the bottom of the step loosened with difficulty. I talked my way through the process to provide Ralph assurance that he wasn't alone. "Ralph, I'm going to pull these bolts and drop the step a little to free your foot. How you doing? Still with me?" I grunted while loosening the first nut and sighed when it broke free. "Got it. That baby's been on there a long time, but I got it. Won't be long now. Hang in there, Ralph. Poor choice of words, sorry." He didn't respond. The second nut, though tight, loosened with less resistance. Why he'd fallen was clear. There was a thick smear of grease on the steps.

I waited for Tuck's return before pulling the bolts free. He came back, wearing shoes and a sweatshirt and carrying towels. He was followed by Margarite and Reggie.

There was no time for introductions. "Good. Glad you're here, Reggie. Tuck, you and Reggie secure Ralph. I'm going to drop the step to free his ankle, but we need to make sure he doesn't topple. Just hold him steady. I know there's not much room in here. You'll have to squeeze inside."

Tuck and his son stood on opposite sides of Ralph. Reggie grasped his belt, front and back. Tuck wrapped himself around Ralph's left leg and held tight. With the bolts pulled on one side of the step, it dropped just enough to free the ankle. As the pressure released, Ralph startled us with a long, slow moan.

"Oh, Ralph," Margarite sighed.

I slid down the steps past Ralph and grasped his shoulders. "Okay guys, I'm going to pull him out. Hang onto him. Easy does it. Reggie, keep an eye on his ankle. Try not to let it hit anything. It's pretty messed up."

We lowered Ralph onto the basement floor. As I wrapped his head with a towel, we heard the ambulance siren and saw Connie standing at the outside basement door. "Connie," I said. "Go out front and direct the paramedics back here, will you?"

The ambulance crew was at Ralph's side in seconds. The two paramedics tended to Ralph, one asking questions at the same time.

"What happened here?" he asked.

"He fell down the stairs," I said.

"What stairs?"

"These," I said, pulling the secret door wide open.

He stood and peered inside the small enclosure and up the staircase and asked, "Where's it go?"

"All the way to the attic," I said.

"What was he doing in there?"

"That's what the hell we'd like to know," Tuck snapped.

"Do you know this man?"

"Hell yes, we know him. But he doesn't belong in this house, I'll tell you that."

"So, you're saying this is a crime scene?"

"That's exactly what I'm saying," Tuck said.

"Now, Tuck," Margarite said. "We don't know for sure. Ralph is a friend."

"Your friend, maybe. Not mine."

I interrupted. "His presence here is suspicious. We live upstairs," I said, motioning toward Connie. "These are the Tuckers. They live downstairs and own the house. There is a weird backstory in play here. Do you know Sergeant Rodrick Bloomfield?"

"Bloomy, sure. Why?"

"Please contact him. He knows what's going on. And, yes, this should be a crime scene until we know more. Tell Bloomfield to come quickly." I didn't mention the grease I'd found on the steps.

"Will do," he said, as he helped roll unconscious Ralph onto a stretcher and carry him out the basement door.

"Who the hell is Bloomfield?" Tuck asked.

"Tuck, better go put on some coffee," I said. "We need to talk."

What Evidence?

14

A T FIVE-THIRTY A.M., THE Tuckers sat on one side of the kitchen table. Reggie sat between his parents. Connie and I sat on the other.

"So, who's this Bloomfield?" Tuck asked.

"He's a detective. A detective who is going to want to hear what you have to say about tonight's visitor and then some. Until he gets here, why don't you tell me what's going on." I knew help was on the way, and it seemed best to stay calm and allow Tuck and Margarite to remain relatively unthreatened for the moment. Still, the night's events required conversation. I spoke slowly and without anger.

"So, we want to know what happened here," I said. "Here's what we know. Someone has had uninvited access to our apartment through the staircase since we moved in, and we think that person has been harassing us the entire time. Plus, Margarite, we are pretty sure you set up the phony ghost hunt to frighten us."

The coffee pot gurgled. Margarite rose to serve. "Take anything in yours?" she asked as she poured and returned to her seat, seemingly untroubled by my accusations.

"Black is fine," I said. Connie said nothing and waved off the offer.

"Let's talk about the spiral staircase. Tuck, you claimed to know nothing about it. Reggie, you told Sergeant Bloomfield both you and your mother knew about it. Obviously, Ralph knew about it. Someone want to tell us what's going on?"

"Please let us handle this as a family matter," Margarite said. "There's much we need to discuss. It's all very private. Plus, I don't think we really owe you an explanation. You're just tenants."

The edges of my soft voice sharpened. "We are tenants who've been illegally harassed since we got here by you or someone you know. Don't kid yourself, Margarite. You can't sidestep this one with a gimlet and a grin. A man about died in your basement just now."

"That wasn't our fault."

"Think that's what Ralph is going to say?"

"I have no idea what he'll say," Margarite said. "He's such a flake."

"I thought he was your friend," Tuck said. "Funny way to talk about a friend. What the hell was that horny little dipshit doing in our house?"

"Let's keep it in the family, Tuck," Margarite said.

"Why should he, Mom?" Reggie said. "Why should he?"

Reggie's interruption quieted the room. That he said anything was surprising, but taking sides with his father was totally unexpected. He awaited an answer, which Margarite wouldn't give.

Connie broke the silence, "We enjoyed your poetry, Reggie. It was good. Do you write often?"

"What are you talking about?"

"Someone left us a wonderful poem about Rebekah Cooperman. It was written by a very clever person. I just figured you did it." Connie's eyes darted from Reggie to Margarite and back as she said it.

"Mom's the poet in the family. Not me." Reggie said.

"Is that true, Margarite?" Connie asked.

"I haven't written in years. I think it's time for you to go," Margarite said as she started to stand.

"Oh, not yet, dear. Things are just getting interesting. Sit down," Tuck instructed. "Answer one question. What was lover-boy-Ralphie doing in our house?"

"How should I know?" she answered, then turned to Connie and me. "I repeat. It's time for you to go."

"We can't leave yet," I said. "We must stay until the police get here. They need to see the evidence I found in the staircase."

"What evidence?" Margarite asked. Twitch, twitch.

"All in good time. All in good time, Margarite. Let's just say you may have something to worry about."

The doorbell rang. Tuck and I both responded. It was Sergeant Bloomfield, accompanied by a young, uniformed policeman named Saunders. Tuck stepped aside, and I opened the door and invited them in.

"Damn, Ron, you got me up early today," Bloomfield said. "Crime scene calls take two of us. This is Officer Saunders. I explained your situation on the ride over. So, what's going on?"

"Great to see you Sergeant," I said, as I shook his hand. "Officer Saunders, nice to meet you. I'm Ron McCall. This is Mr. Tucker. He's our landlord and Reggie's father. There are people in the kitchen you'll want to talk to. We've had quite a night." Tuck and Bloomfield and Officer Saunders followed me to the kitchen.

"You know Connie, and you know Reggie. This is Margarite, Tuck's wife."

"They told me you had someone stuck in your staircase. What's that about?" Bloomfield asked.

Tuck sat down. Bloomfield, Saunders, and I remained standing while I told them about our bloody night with Ralph. "He's off to the hospital, and Margarite wants to keep it a family matter. That's not possible because of what I found when we freed him. Please join me in the basement, Sergeant. You may need this." I handed him my headlamp. "Okay for Officer Saunders to hold down the fort here?"

"Sure. How long's this going to take."

"Not long."

"Saunders, keep these people company, will you?" Bloomfield said.

"I've got it, Sergeant."

"So, what's the big secret, Ron?" Bloomfield asked as we went down the basement stairs from the kitchen.

"Someone greased the stairs. There's a thick coat of clear grease on the step that took him down. That means someone wanted him stopped, injured or dead."

"Really. Let's have a look."

We entered the basement, and I guided him to the spiral staircase. Bloomfield stepped past the knot of bloody towels lying on the floor in front of the secret doorway and swung the door open. He stepped in and around the puddle of drying blood and looked up.

"Look about four or five steps up. It's the one I loosened. That step and at least two above it have grease all over them. You'll see it," I said. I stood directly behind him.

"Damn, that would give you a tumble. The stairs are steep anyway. Slip on some grease and there's no way to go but down. Doesn't make sense. If someone was trying to spook you, why would someone else sabotage the whole thing with a trap like this?"

"I think Margarite and Ralph were partners in crime. They tried to frighten us and others who've lived here. I have no idea why, and I don't have any idea who greased the stairs. Could have been Margarite if she'd fallen out with Ralph. It could have been Tuck. I think he despises Ralph for bedding Margarite, but he claims he knew nothing about the hidden staircase. It could have been Reggie. He knew about the staircase, but why would he want to harm Ralph?"

"Or it could have been you. You knew about the staircase and had motive. Did you grease the staircase, Ron?"

His question caught me totally off guard. "Hell no! You think I would …."

"I had to ask," he said. "You understand. Let's go back upstairs. Anything else I should know?"

Still flummoxed from being considered a suspect, I answered slowly as we walked toward the stairs. "Only that we think Margarite wrote the Rebekah poem and we caught her cheating during the ghost hunt. She set the whole thing up to frighten us."

"Cheating?"

"I'll tell you later," I whispered, as we entered the kitchen.

"Coffee smells good. Got an extra cup?" Bloomfield asked as he pulled up an empty chair on our side of the table. He turned it backward and straddled it. "What Ron just showed me gives us some things to ponder. Coffee might help."

Margarite didn't budge. Connie got up, poured Bloomfield's coffee, offered some to Saunders, who remained standing at the kitchen entrance. He declined. We both returned to our seats alongside Bloomfield.

"Thank you," Bloomfield said. He rested his folded arms across the chair back and paused long enough to survey the Tucker family with eyes that left no place to hide. "Looks like someone intentionally tried to harm Ralph, and we have a crime to solve.

"Saunders, go down and tape the basement. Both entrance doors and the door on the north wall, which opens to the spiral staircase. Be careful where you step."

"Crime?" Margarite asked.

"Yes, indeed. There's grease all over the steps down there. Any idea who could've put it there?"

"Tuck, you son of a bitch. I can't believe it. You rotten, unforgiving son of a bitch," Margarite said. Her scowl was amplified by a squirting surge of saliva, which landed on Reggie. He winced and wiped, but it was good that he sat between his parents.

Tuck threw his hands in the air. "Hold the phone there, sweet cheeks. I had no idea the staircase was there. You know as well as I do, I've spent all of twenty minutes in the basement in the thirty years we've lived here. Every tool down there came with the house. Something needed done, I hired it done. How would I know about some secret doorway and staircase? How in the hell did you find out about it? That's the better question."

Margarite started to speak but stopped.

"Go ahead, Margarite." Bloomfield said. "What were you about to say?"

Margarite took a deep, stalling breath, which exploded in my face. "You did it, McCall! I knew you were a treacherous shit the day I met you," She cast an accusing finger toward me. "I don't know what Ralph was doing on those stupid stairs, but somehow, you did. And you tried to kill him. You make me sick!"

As ridiculous as it was, Margarite's accusation landed hard, and I sat in stunned silence. Connie came to my rescue.

"Yes, Margarite, you are sick." Connie said. "And, yes, we knew about the staircase." Connie's reaction was calm and sharp. "Unlike the parade of tenants you've harassed over the years, we found the stairs, but we didn't grease them. We called the police. So, here we sit, Margarite, waiting for your pathetic answers. Why don't you put some gin in your coffee and start talking?"

"I'll ask again, Margarite," Tuck said. "How'd you know about the stairs? How'd you know, and how long have you known? You sure as hell didn't build them yourself."

Angry pride seemed to overcome caution. Margarite blurted, "Yes I did. I built them!" She spoke as the exalted keeper of the Cooperman House. "I managed the whole goddamned apartment conversion. Remember? While you were traveling around the fricking world looking for bamboo place mats to sell to Walmart, I built the whole damned thing. I hired the architect, approved the plans, and hired the contractors. All you did was cosign the papers between trips to Bangkok and Mozambique, you lazy blowhard."

"I kept you in the chips, didn't I? Who do you think paid for your little architectural excursion? Took a lot of place mats to pay for your fancy spiral staircase. Why in the world would you do that?"

"At the time, I had plans to convert the entire attic, not just the little bedroom. We needed a fire escape."

"Fire escape, my ass. That's a fire trap," Tuck countered. "You've always relished the Rebekah Cooperman story. I think you knew exactly what you were going to do with the staircase. So, why'd you decide to kill Ralph?"

Margarite screamed, "I didn't! Why would I? I love Ralph!" Her head ratcheted to her right before she bowed it, apparently relieved at what she had just said.

Bloomfield stood, allowing his authoritative presence to calm the room. "Okay, gang. Let's be civil if we can. At least slow down a little. So, Margarite, when did you decide to use the staircase for paranormal entertainment?"

Margarite's acerbic spittle had turned to tears. Connie retrieved a box of tissues from the counter and slid it hard across the table to Margarite. Margarite stopped it with an upturned palm, frowned at Connie, and grabbed a tissue and dabbed. She looked up at Bloomfield, secure in her renewed rage. "Entertainment? It wasn't entertainment. It was my attempt to get that exasperating blowhard out of my life. You try living with an arrogant buffoon whose inane jabber is so full of Moroccan camel shit that you have to hold your breath to be in the same room with him."

"So, you terrorized your tenants to get Tuck to leave?" Bloomfield asked. "I don't get it."

"Yes, ol' King Tut Tuck. I figured if we scared enough people away, he'd get tired of having people come and go. He'd want out. He's too goddamned important to be an apartment manager."

She took a long, slow breath and a wild-eyed scan of our side of the table. Then she exhaled a torrent of venomous loathing. "He'd sell this house and buy a mountain tavern where he'd sit with his ass-kissing cronies and brag about his travels. Oh, he loves to tell stories. Can't you just hear him? 'Ah, yes, gather round boys. Let me tell you about rhino-horn aphrodisiacs from Viet Nam, pure cocaine from Colombia, and teenaged whores from Bangkok.' They'd lap it up, and he'd just keep talking. He'd even buy another round just to hear himself talk. Of course, to do all that he'd need to sell the house."

She leaned forward and turned toward Tuck, looking him square in the eyes. "Well, surprise, surprise. You couldn't sell the house if you wanted to because it's in my name. That's the paper you signed just before you ran off to chase geodes in Brazil, you naive, self-important idiot. Don't you get it? I wanted you out of my life and out of the way. Ralph and I could have the place to ourselves. With all that planning, why would I try to I kill him?"

No one ventured to guess. The moment of silence lingered. I looked at Connie, who returned my glance with a long, slow blink.

"Then who did?" I asked.

Tuck looked around the table and Margarite sneered straight ahead. Reggie wrapped his hands around his coffee cup and stared at it. The only sound was Officer Saunders coming up the basement steps.

"Come on folks. Talk to us. Two of you admit to knowing about the staircase. One of you has an obvious motive for harming Ralph. Who put the grease on the steps?" Bloomfield pressured. The silence continued.

"We will get to the bottom of this," Bloomfield said. "Yes, we will. For now, I've got to get you out of here, Reggie. You're on house arrest, and this is a crime scene. You can't stay here. Stand up and put your hands behind your back." Bloomfield cuffed Reggie and turned to Officer Saunders. "Take Reggie to the car and wait for me. I'm going to wrap things up here, and then we'll take him downtown. After that, we'll have a visit with Ralph, provided he can talk."

Officer Saunders cupped his strong hand around Reggie's left elbow and began to escort him toward the doorway. Reggie took one step forward, stopped, and spoke. "I did it. I greased the steps."

"What?" Margarite asked. "You did what?

Reggie faced his mother. Handcuffs kept him from gesturing, and it didn't matter. His biting words were enough. "Mom, I've known about you and Ralph since I was fifteen. It's the reason our family went to hell. I hated you for it. I also knew about your supernatural tricks. You always spoke in front of me like I wasn't there. In your eyes, I was a piece of goddamned furniture."

"But you fought tooth and nail with your dad, not me," Margarite said.

"Yeah, but I didn't hate him. I hated his cowardice. He talks big and loud and long. He has an opinion on everything from popcorn to Aztec toilet paper. He's full of information, but he's a coward. He knew about your cheating and did nothing about it. That's why I left. I was in between, and I just wanted out. Believe me, not having to live with Dad's missing backbone and your malicious cheating was a huge relief."

"You think he was faithful to me during his far-flung travels? You've got another think coming," Margarite snapped.

"Okay, okay," Bloomfield interrupted. "Your marital difficulties are fascinating, but they are not important right now. Reggie, how'd you know Ralph was going to make an upstairs visit last night?"

"I didn't know he would do it last night, but I knew he'd do it. I heard Mom talking to him on the phone. Like I said, to her I'm a worn-out footstool," Reggie said.

He turned and addressed his mother, "Mom, I heard you talking. You admitted the McCalls were tough to frighten, but you thought one more good nudge would get them out of here. You told Ralph he'd find a vial of chicken blood in a coffee can on the workbench. He was to place a clean sheet of paper in Ron's typewriter, type 'Coming Soon' on it, and then dribble blood across the note and the typewriter. I heard your instructions, but I didn't hear when. So, you see, I didn't know last night was the night. But grease is grease, slick today and slick tomorrow."

Reggie paused and looked at Bloomfield. "I just wanted the whole damned charade to stop," he said. "I wasn't out to harm Ralph. I was trying to block her devious bullshit once and for all. If Ralph got hurt in the process, so be it. He's even more spineless than Dad."

"You thankless, spoiled, little shit. My precious, sensitive, mistreated Reggie. Poor baby," Margarite paused to reload. "I guess we all have regrets. But you, Reggie, are an absolute disappointment. You're a pitiful, embarrassing loser. Sergeant, get him out of my house before I puke!" Margarite said.

"Oh, I'll get him out of here, but you're coming with me. Stand up, Margarite. You are under arrest for conspiring to break and enter and personal harassment."

"What are you talking about?" Margarite barked.

"I'm talking about your lack of respect for other people's space and general wellbeing. Of course, this will depend on Ron and Connie's willingness to press charges. What do you think, Ron? Connie?"

I looked at Connie. She spoke first, "When you asked us earlier, we said we simply wanted the stupid ghostly visits to stop. But after learning about the treachery behind this mess, I think we should press charges. What do you think, Ron?"

"I agree. I'm sure you'll find a way to kick us out of here, whatever we do. But what you did was despicable, Margarite. Chicken blood! Are you kidding me? Chicken blood! If we leave, you can be sure we'll remain close enough to see you in court."

"I'll need a written statement from you two. Can you do that?" Bloomfield asked.

"Sure," I said.

"Simply tell us what happened to you. Don't speculate about motives. That's not your job. I'm betting there's more to this story than Margarite's told us. But crimes were committed, and we know who committed them. That's all we need for now," Bloomfield instructed.

"Stand up, Margarite. Put your hands behind your back," Bloomfield said. He retrieved a wrist restraint from his jacket pocket and pulled it tight around Margarite's narrow wrists and stated her Miranda rights.

I didn't want the conversation to stop. Margarite stood before me as remorseless evil. She'd kept Tuck sedated with martinis when he was home and found another man when he was gone. She'd tied her son in emotional knots for years. She'd even manipulated and victimized her lover, not to mention her thoughtless abuse of unsuspecting tenants.

Maybe one day I'd be able to explore the exonerating corners of her twisted personality. But not now. I wanted her to squirm through a hammering summary of her sins. Of course, there was no time for that. But there was time for one final shot.

"Margarite, just so you'll know, your monofilament trickery fooled no one. Did you really think you could jerk a fishing line and conjure up the spirit of Rebekah Cooperman?"

"Well, aren't you the smart one?" she asked. Her tortured face smoothed into a friendly smile, which seemed to welcome me as a kindred spirit. "Those paranormal douche bags would have crapped their pants, wouldn't they?"

Eager to Believe

15

BLOOMFIELD CALLED MATTY ON the day of Ralph's arrest to inform her she'd be without a pharmacist for a while. He told her Ralph was under arrest for breaking and entering and was hospitalized because of a disturbance at the Tucker's house. She waited all day to hear more, and when she didn't, she called us. Connie answered.

"Yes, I know what happened to Ralph," Connie said. "It's a long story. The bottom line is this: Ralph is in the hospital after a fall down a secret staircase at Cooperman House. He and Margarite Tucker used the hidden stairs to frighten renters with bogus Rebekah Cooperman appearances for years."

Connie's off-the-cuff summary only whetted Matty's appetite, and there was too much story for a business hours phone conversation. We met with Matty at the store at closing time.

She locked the door behind us after we entered, turned off all but one bank of fluorescent lights, and invited us back to the spartan break room, where we sat at an oval table in front of a noisy refrigerator. She minced no words and asked, "What the hell are you talking about? He fell down a secret staircase while pretending to be Rebekah Cooperman?"

Connie and I filled in the blanks, with special emphasis on the night of the arrest. "Did you know Ralph and Margarite were an item?" I asked.

"I had no idea. No idea at all. And I sure as hell didn't know he was the ghost haunting your apartment. We've worked together for years. I just knew him as a quiet, almost timid, bachelor pharmacist. Still water runs deep, they say."

"Deep water can be treacherous," Connie said.

Matty paused, looked down, then up at us. "The sneaky little bastard. He enjoyed a good ghost story as much as I did. In fact, when one of the renters shared a story with me, he relished its retelling. He'd ask me for every detail, then he'd eagerly chuckle his way through the story, shaking his head in feigned disbelief. Boy, did I misread him. I was so eager to believe all that supernatural crap I welcomed his deceitful attention. Appears I'm as naive as he is dishonest. Damn, I feel so stupid."

"You shouldn't. He and Margarite fooled a lot of people for a long time. Fooled us too, until Lawrence helped us find the spiral staircase. Lawrence is the hero here, and he doesn't even know it."

"He's about the only person in the neighborhood you can trust, seems like." Matty said.

"What are you going to do about a pharmacist?" I asked.

"We'll get some temporary help. That'll be no problem. Parting with Ralph will be odd. He's been here forever, and that may count for something. But I can't see anyone wanting to keep him after this."

"Do you think anyone will see him as a victim?" Connie asked.

"Victim of his own need to be victimized. Why else would he hang in there as Margarite's plaything for all that time?"

"I don't know," Connie said. "I do know I'm glad this ghost nonsense is all over. We've told you all we know. We'll let you know what happens next."

Matty walked us to the front of the store to let us out. "Thank you for talking with me. Right now, I just don't know what to think. Digesting all this will take time." Matty said.

"Time well spent, I think," Connie replied.

Stubborn Souls

16

B LOOMFIELD CALLED TO SEE if we had completed our written statement and to give us an update. As we expected, Margarite and Reggie remained in jail. The good news was Ralph was awake and healing, though still hospitalized. It appeared his head injury had not caused permanent damage, although they'd have to rebuild his mangled ankle.

Our document was ready. I had typed it on my trusty Underwood the night before, tucked the three double-spaced pages inside a manila envelope, and set it aside on the kitchen table. It lay there quietly between us as we sipped our morning coffee. We'd stuck to the facts as Bloomfield requested, but the document seemed shallow, even disrespectful of Margarite's complexity. She was, and would remain, unforgettable. At first, she was simply an eccentric oddity whom we viewed with ambivalent affection. Making fun of Margarite was fun. Now, we understood more about the depth of her twisted weirdness.

Tuck was also faced with a new reality. Connie was first to step back far enough to realize it. "What should we do about

Tuck?" Connie asked. "In many ways, he's as much of a victim as we are."

"I suppose he is, but there's not much we can do about that. He is certainly not going to want to talk to us. We just caused his world to fall apart."

"Think about it. We did him a favor. His life was a lie before we arrived," Connie said. "And it could be that you're just the person he should talk to. You saw him in the middle of his humiliation. If he knows you see past it, maybe he can too. Go see how he's doing."

"Me? You want me to go see him alone?"

"Yep. Man to man."

I liked Tuck from the beginning. His brassiness was refreshing, and I remembered the surprising fondness I felt toward him during our first conversation. I glanced at the manila envelope. As thin as it was, it was a new beginning for all of us. Connie was right. I'd try to speak with Tuck.

I rang the doorbell and waited. I rang it again and was about to go back upstairs when Tuck opened the door. "Hello. I just wanted to see how you're doing. Have time to talk a moment?"

"Sure, Ron. Come on in," he said, as he tightened the sash on his kimono. "I was just getting dressed. Forgive my casual attire. Coffee's fresh. Want a cup?"

"Sure. That'd be great."

I followed him into the kitchen. Tuck poured and said, "Let's go back to the living room. It's more comfortable." As I followed him, I admired the intricate detail of his robe. The tiger's tail, the flowers, and the foliage swayed with his back as he walked. It seemed the best place to begin.

"That's a gorgeous robe, Tuck," I said as we sat in front of his fireplace "I've never seen anything quite like it. It's amazing."

"Thank you. It was a gift from a friend during my last trip to Japan. He gave me one for Margarite too. It had fire-breathing dragons on it. She didn't wear it much. I don't think she appreciated how perfect it was for her."

I wanted to laugh. I only smiled.

"What's up, Ron," Tuck asked.

"We shared a night of revelations, didn't we?"

"Revelations? I think I prefer bullshit."

"I hear you. But the more I thought about it, the more it seemed you got the worst of it. I mean, when the dust settled, you were left here alone. All alone. Are you doin' okay?"

"I'm fine, Ron. I'm fine. Nice of you to ask though. I'm fine."

"Were you surprised how the night unfolded?" I asked.

Surprised? Yeah, I was surprised at that goofy staircase. I was surprised Reggie had the balls to do what he did. I was surprised pasty-faced Ralph was still smelling around Margarite, but I wasn't surprised at her treachery. Margarite is all about Margarite. Always has been."

"So, you knew about Margarite's affair with Ralph."

"Knew about it years ago and thought it was over years ago," Tuck said as he leaned forward, placed his hands on his knees, and stared at the floor. Then he looked up and said, "I was crazy angry at first. But I really couldn't blame her. I was gone a lot. It's all very circular. I was gone because she was such a hard person to live with. My import business gave me freedom, marvelous freedom. I met people from dozens of different countries and cultures. People with lives I could never have imagined if I'd stayed home. I was a citizen of the world, and I loved every minute of it." Tuck hesitated and smiled, "Sounds lofty, doesn't it? The truth is, as great as it was, it was all accidental."

"Accidental?" I asked.

"Yes. None of it would have happened if I hadn't fled from Margarite's incessant, underhanded neediness. But Reggie was right about one thing. I ran instead of dealing with it."

"But you stood your ground pretty well the other night around your kitchen table."

"I had little choice. There was so much crap rolling at me I had to stand and fight. I mean, I had to deal with Margarite's lies, a ghost, a pip-squeak pharmacist, a half-crazed son, and a pushy detective."

"And Connie and me, of course." I paused and asked, "Her paranormal schemes? You had no inkling?"

"Oh, hell no. Probably should have, but I didn't. Looking back, most of the supernatural complaints occurred when I was home, which was her plan, of course. If someone left on their own while I was gone, she'd go on and on about it when I got home, adding imagined detail of another ghostly visit. Yes, I should have known."

"Don't be too hard on yourself. Her scheme was totally un-believable. Who could have guessed what she was up to?"

"And what do you think she was up to?" Tuck asked.

"Well, I guess she wanted you gone."

Tuck smiled, looked me straight in the eye, and said, "That was just smoke, pure, unadulterated smoke. Margarite is patient and calculating, but even she wouldn't spend all that time trying to clear the way for Ralphie-boy. She had no long-range plan. She was simply having fun. Ralph was just an excuse to cover her maliciousness. I mean, who the hell would want to share a house with a wuss like Ralph? Not even Margarite, I don't think. She'd rather just toy with him, and anyone else who'll let her."

Tuck stood slowly, circled his chair, and stepped toward the bookshelves. He picked up his coveted Brazilian geode, polished the slick face of the half rock against his sleeve, and handed it to me, "Light can add interest to this beauty. Hold it in the light and turn it a little. Watch the colors dance."

I held it slightly above my head so the window's light could awaken its colors. As I rotated the rock, its clustered segments of orange, opal, and purple revolved in a sympathetic ballet, each allowing the others equal time on center stage. "Nice," I said.

"Most people are the same way. When seen in a different light, something magical happens. They surprise us. That's why we love them." He took the geode from me, placed it back on the shelf, and returned to his chair. "But when the dancing is done, the colors return to their fixed positions. Each is there as it was before, well defined, familiar, and reassuring . . . another reason to love them.

"That's not the way of things with Margarite. Sometime along the way, her delicate stripe of purple crystals became an indelible core of putrid, black marrow and didn't change. I'm not sure I'd call her a psychopath, but you can fit her portion of empathy inside a thimble. Our unfortunate renters became a parade of unsuspecting characters in her private supernatural theater. And, like any serial criminal, she could pull the curtain for the next act whenever she wanted a little sadistic chuckle. What did your detective call it? Paranormal entertainment, wasn't it? And that's what it was, and all for an audience of one."

Tuck paused and smiled. "Then you came along, and you didn't scare. You two stubborn souls dug in and wouldn't budge. Poor, poor Margarite. She'd met her match. Plus, I was home full time to pester her. Margarite went batshit crazy, started writing poems, and hiring ghost hunters and was undone when her boyfriend slipped on the grease."

"I knew she was behind it all when she sat in the guilty chair," I said. Then I explained how we caught her trying to bring Rebekah Cooperman out of hiding with fishing line and a rolling geode. Of course, I also explained how we discovered her trickiness.

"Ha!" Tuck exclaimed and slapped his knee. "Now that's funny! That's downright wonderful. She was undone by someone as devious as she is. You must be kindred spirits," Tuck said and laughed.

It was great to see him laugh, but I wished I'd kept the story to myself.

"Sounds like you're willing let her sit in jail a while if it comes to that."

"Yep." Tuck said. He hesitated and pursed his lips as if he had more to say about his future with Margarite. Then he said, "How's your coffee, Ron? Need a warmup?"

"No thank you. I should be going. Thanks for talking with me. Please don't get lonely down here. Need help of any kind, call us. We're right upstairs."

"Thank you, Ron." Tuck stood to see me out. "One more thing. You suggested we'd want you to move because of all this. Well, that's not true. You can stay as long as you like. I spoke with my attorney. Margarite's phony deed doesn't mean squat. She'll have no say about who stays and who goes. Only leave if you want to. I'd love to have you stay."

"Thank you, Tuck. I am very happy to hear that. Connie will be too."

I was glad I'd spoken with Tuck. Our conversation helped both of us, I think. He validated his thoughts by speaking them, and my unsettling anger toward Margarite was greatly diminished. Only disgust remained.

Bloomfield picked up our written statement later that afternoon.

Yonder

17

A s the dust settled, our lives slowed to a more comfortable and predictable pace. Connie concentrated on teaching, and I concentrated on school. Glazier's Pharmacy had a new pharmacist, Matty was as congenial and helpful as before. Lawrence still preferred Butterfinger and Cherry Mash candy bars, and he became an important part of our routine.

We spoke with Lawrence almost every day as he walked past the house. I continued to take him to Helping Hands Workshop when his mother asked. Sometimes, he'd even knock on the door and just want to talk. We were always glad to see him, and if the time wasn't right, he understood. We were sure his mother had instructed him not to become a bother, because he always began his unplanned visits with a polite inquiry. "You busy now?" he'd ask. Usually, we asked him in.

If we planned to drive to the mountains, we often invited him to join us. Sometimes he did. During the summer, the Rocky Mountains become a tourist playground. We tried to avoid most of the touristy options, except for the day we took Lawrence on a trail ride. Buck, the stable keeper, assured us he had a mount suitable for him. The slow, sure-footed, old white horse with a speckled rump was named Sugar. Lawrence fell in love with Sugar and with riding and he didn't fuss at all when Buck touched his leg and patted him on the back as he helped him mount old Sugar. We called ahead and reserved Sugar for Lawrence three additional times that summer. It was such an easy, undemanding friendship and stood in stark contrast to the Rebekah Cooperman confusion, which we were glad to leave behind.

Our neighbor Art Mingus had a tougher time without Rebekah. He was a man of contradictions. When our ghost hunt began, he was one of the first to assure us that Rebekah Cooperman was dead and gone. But after the truth was revealed, he couldn't let her rest. He mentioned her every time we spoke and had an insatiable appetite for details during the trials.

He seemed satisfied with the outcomes and was particularly delighted to know that Tuck got his wish. Margarite was forever banned from Cooperman House. She would also spend eight months in jail and was fined $3,000. Ralph got off easier. He claimed he was the unfortunate victim of his agreeable, dutiful personality. That may have helped some, but he was given a lighter sentence mostly because of his injuries and because Margarite was the obvious mastermind of the paranormal scheme. He'd spend six months in jail, was fined $1,000, and lost his job at Glaziers Pharmacy. Reggie, charged with felony assault and robbery for his attack on Lawrence and reckless endangerment for greasing the stairs, went to the state penitentiary for four years and would be on mandatory parole for five years after release.

Even a year later, Art couldn't contain his lingering Rebekah obsession. During Lawrence's thirty-third birthday party, which occurred three weeks before we moved, he mentioned her. Lawrence's home was full of company. Sam was there. Two

Helping Hands friends were there. Mrs. Stroud's sister and daughter came down from Boulder. Tuck even popped in for a moment.

Mrs. Stroud entered the room with the birthday cake ablaze. She placed the frosted inferno in front of Lawrence, who immediately blew out the candles with three enormous breaths. We all broke into a round applause and *Happy Birthday*. It was fun to watch Lawrence being loved, and we were all better for having participated.

Art stood beside me, holding an empty punch cup. "A great day for Lawrence, isn't it?" Art asked. Then he lowered his voice to a whisper and said, "Too bad Rebekah couldn't be here."

"Oh, she's here. She just passed by. Didn't you feel her?" I asked. I'd grown used to his benign fixation and decided the least I could do was feed it a little. He'd have to find a new Rebekah sounding board when Cooperman House had new tenants.

My two years at Denver University had flown by. I'd accepted a job with the Federal Bureau of Investigation and was to begin training in Quantico, Virginia in June. We weren't just changing addresses. We were leaving friends. We'd told everyone except Lawrence. We wanted to postpone his goodbye as long as we could. His mother agreed to break the news to Lawrence a couple of days before moving day and to delay his trip to Helping Hands on that morning so we could join him at their home to say goodbye. She and Tuck had a better idea.

The eighteen-wheeler came about eight a.m. and parked in front of Cooperman House. The moving men noisily dragged the metal loading ramp from the trailer and locked it in place. Because we didn't have much to move, we were sharing space in the truck with others moving east. The truck was loaded by nine o'clock. Connie and I stood by the cab with the driver. I signed the papers, and we turned toward our empty apartment, dreading the short walk to Lawrence's house. It was a walk we didn't have to take. We were greeted by Tuck and Lawrence, standing on the front porch of Cooperman House.

Tuck waited for us to reach the porch and for the noise of the departing truck to subside before he spoke. "Well, now. Two days from now you'll be neighbors with the president. Tell him hello for me, will you?"

"I'll give him your best," I said. I couldn't look at Lawrence, but I could feel my eyes welling and my throat tighten.

"We're here is to wish you well and to send you off right," Tuck said. "That's important to both of us. Especially Lawrence."

I looked at Connie before I looked at Lawrence. She was already crying. She tried to smile through her tears, but her quivering lips wouldn't give way to a grin. I knew I'd soon be in worse shape than she was. I looked at Lawrence. He stood expressionless, his arms snug against his sides, with his hands fisted. I remembered his aversion to touch, but his odd, rigid position seemed like an invitation to hug him. That's what I did. I embraced him with a gentle, but increasingly tight hug. He relaxed in my grasp. I whispered in his ear through tears, "I love you, Lawrence."

"Coop, Coop, Coop," Lawrence said. "Lawrence love Coop."

"Bells and chimes are going to ring," I chanted.

"Mamie Eisenhower, Mamie Eisenhower, Mamie Eisenhower," he responded.

I released him and stood back and smiled. One pearl-sized tear rolled down his pink cheek.

"Connie Coop, Connie Coop, Connie Coop," Lawrence said.

Connie moved forward and stood beside me. She reached for his right hand. He avoided contact and placed his hand in his pants pocket. He withdrew it quickly, holding a pristine

1953 Corvette in his chubby hand. "Connie Coop keep. Connie Coop keep," he demanded.

She took the toy car from him, lightly touching his hand. "I will," she said. "Always."

"Well, Lawrence," Tuck said. "We'd better let these people get going. They've got to beat that big ol' truck to Virginia, and it has a head start 'em. Come on, I'll take you to work and tell them why you're a little late."

"Okay," Lawrence said. "Go see Sam. Go see Sam." Tuck and Lawrence walked around the house to Tuck's car.

Tuck was masterful. He'd made the dreaded goodbye sweet, unforgettable, and over before we knew it. In fact, when we went back upstairs for our bags and a final walk-through, we realized we'd forgotten to give Lawrence his gift. It was a framed picture of the four of us, Connie, me, Lawrence, and Sugar. Lawrence sat mounted on Sugar, reins in his hands, which rested on the saddle horn like he'd been riding all his life. Connie and I stood alongside, grinning. We gave it to his mother before we began our drive across the country.

Because we towed Connie's car, the trip to Quantico was slow. We didn't mind. The extra road time was welcome therapy.

———

Four years later, I'm still with the FBI. We have our own small, but comfortable, home near Quantico, and we often think about our days at Cooperman House. Our nicknames live on between the two of us, and we still exchange Christmas cards with Lawrence and his mother and with Tuck. Tuck always includes a note. Last Christmas he updated us on the spiral staircase:

> *"I finally had Margarite's staircase sealed off, top and bottom. It took two solid days of dusty hammering. I'm surprised it didn't awaken Rebekah, but I saw nothing of her. If I had, I'm sure she would've sung*

your praises for setting her free. I would've told her I
felt the same way."

His Christmas greetings always made us smile. So does the sassy, little white sportscar with a red interior and no external door handles, which sits on my office credenza, alongside Connie's picture. People often ask about it. To car buffs, it's a shining example of American automotive ingenuity. Even people who know nothing of the car's trendsetting importance notice it. They wonder if I'm a collector or if I've restored a full-sized car. I usually just tell them it's a gift from a good friend and let it go at that. Other times, special times, if I think the person has a playful imagination and time to listen, I let them take a little spin in the Corvette, which usually leads to very good ghost story.

END

www.ingramcontent.com/pod-product-compliance
Lightning Source LLC
Chambersburg PA
CBHW070821250626
47170CB00006B/2183